UNLEASH ME: WEDDING

CHRISTINA ROSS

For my friends and my family,
and especially for my readers, who mean the world to me.

Your support has been unparalleled, and I appreciate it more than
you know.

INTRODUCTION

Author's note: When it comes to officiating at a wedding, I'm no priest or minister. Going into this book, though, I realized I needed to know all the things a priest would say to Lisa and Tank as they got married. Clueless, I took to the Internet and found lots of sites that gave me a good idea of what is generally said during a wedding ceremony. In that process, I found that much of it seemed like a script to me, with few variations. Please know that to get this wedding right, I leaned hard on those scripts—sometimes literally using them word-for-word. Other times, I changed the words to suit the wedding in question. For reference purposes, I particularly used the following script, and I offer it to you here in full disclosure: **http://bit.ly/2rr98Uv**. Otherwise in this book, the words are all mine.

1

New York City
Mid-February

"YOU'RE SCREWED."

It wasn't my best friend, Jennifer Wenn, who'd said what I already knew in my heart to be true. Instead, Barbara Blackwell had spoken those words—not that their coming from her had surprised me.

She was sitting opposite me—decked out in one of her many black Chanel suits, her dark plumb of a bob hanging stylishly over her right cheek, a solitaire diamond glimmering in each earlobe. She picked over her salad as if she didn't have a care in the world, despite how dark my own looked at that moment.

The three of us were having dinner at the Milling Room, a terrific restaurant on Manhattan's Upper West Side that was *the* place to go. It wasn't just the restaurant's warm, stylish ambience that drew people in—the Milling Room had once been an old hotel lobby before it had been transformed into a chic tavern with gray brick walls, a domed glass ceiling, and dark wooden flooring that gleamed. It was also because its chef had a Michelin star, and the food was something to savor and seek out.

Getting a table here was beyond difficult—never mind snagging a *great* table. But since Jennifer had decided the three of us needed to nail down the details of my wedding tonight, she had been the one to phone in the reservation. And because Jennifer happened to be Jennifer Wenn of Wenn Enterprises—a woman this city had come to champion as one of its own—we naturally had the best table in the house, which overlooked the entire dining area from the back far right of the room.

Despite our beautiful surroundings, I sipped my martini with irritation as I watched Blackwell stab her fork squarely into the middle of a piece of cucumber before she lifted her eyes to me—and then leveled me with a penetrating gaze.

"I mean it, darling—you're screwed."

"Seriously, Barbara?" I said. "Screwed?"

"Oh, please," she said, her fork poised in the air as she waved the cucumber this way and that in front of my face. "As you know very well, all the best churches are booked for the month of June, as are the best places to have your reception. So, tell me—what don't you understand? We have called literally *everyone* in this city, and despite our collective influence, it's clear that nothing is available."

"It's infuriating," I said.

"That's because you're still in denial. Lisa, you need to listen to me now and suck in this bit of information like the cold gust of Arctic wind that it is—unless you want to lower your standards and choose less-desirable locations, such as a ghetto or an alleyway, you are not getting married in

Manhattan in June. So, allow me to repeat—you're screwed."

"Oh, come on," Jennifer said to Blackwell as she reached for my hand and squeezed it in her lap. "Don't be so hard on her."

"If Lisa and Tank had thought this through, they would have set a date the moment they got engaged—you know, over two years ago—and everything would be good to go at this point. We would have secured a church, and we would have had our choice of reception halls. But as far as I know, all Lisa and Tank have been able to book is a honeymoon in Bora Bora—and good luck when it comes to that, Lisa, because if this wedding of yours doesn't come together, you're only going there for a vacation and not a honeymoon."

"Ugh!" I said. "Fine. What am I supposed to do?"

"The only thing you can do—move the date," Blackwell said.

"Move the date? I can't do that to Tank. Everyone heard him on Christmas Eve—he sees me as a June bride."

"He does," Jennifer said.

"I mean, right? And because he's so excited about the wedding, he's taking four weeks off from work so we can not only have our dream wedding but also our extended honeymoon, where we plan to sex it up."

"How perfectly demure of you."

"Look, lady, just so we're on the same page, I can tell you this—ever since Tank set a date, the sex between us has been amazing. I mean, just last night he was holding me off the floor as if I were as weightless as a rag doll while he kept pounding in and out of me. I swear to you, it was enough to turn me into an unhinged, screaming, wanton sex goddess."

"Another martini, ladies?"

I turned my head and saw our handsome waiter standing at my left. How long had he been standing there? Long enough for me to finish my sordid tale of discovering new positions with Tank? I looked for signs that he'd heard what I'd just said, but I couldn't see any.

"Well!" Blackwell said. "How absolutely revealing of you, Lisa. Tales of sexual acrobatics even before we've had the tuna tartare. Tell me," she said, looking up at our waiter, "is she the first one to defile this place? If she is, you can feel free to confide in me..."

"Excuse me?" he said.

"Oh, I see," she said in a low voice. "We're talking in code right now, aren't we, my dear boy? How very covert of you. How absolutely 007. That said, I have to wonder if those around us heard her—"

I had to stop her from running her mouth, so I piped up and ordered another martini. "Jennifer? Barbara?" I asked.

"One is enough for me," Blackwell said. "Although I wouldn't mind a glass of ice right now."

The man furrowed his brow at her. "Just ice? Would you like some mineral water or some—"

"Just the ice," Blackwell said with a wave of her hand. "Biting down on the cubes soothes me."

"I'll join my friend and also have another martini," Jennifer said.

"But should you?" Blackwell said. "I mean—think of the calories alone, Jennifer."

"The calories?" Jennifer said. "I believe I've taken off the baby weight in record time, Barbara. It's only been eight weeks since I had Aiden, and I've literally worked my ass off to get back to the size I was before I got pregnant. Tonight is the first night I've had the opportunity to go out with you and Lisa since I gave birth, so yes—I *will* have another."

As the waiter nodded and left, I watched Blackwell push aside her salad before she shot Jennifer a look.

"How's Helga working out?" she asked. "Still good?"

"It's only been a week since she agreed to be our full-time nanny, but as quirky as she is, I do like her. And Aiden has really taken to her. I hired her early to make sure she's comfortable in the apartment and with Aiden before I go back to work—which is only four weeks from now."

"Excuse me," I interjected. "Need I remind either of you that my wedding is only four months away? Can we please get back to focusing on that? It *is* why we're here, after all."

"Look," Blackwell said, "why even bother if you're not willing to listen to reason? I've already told you that you're shit out of luck when it comes to getting married in June in Manhattan. Either you agree to move the date to next year, or you need to work something else out. I don't see another way around this, and because of that, I also don't see why we need to keep harping about it if you're not willing to bend."

"It's not that I'm unwilling to bend—"

"Oh, please."

"I'm not. I'm just trying to honor Tank. He set that date, and that date is when we are going to get married."

"Then I suggest you broach the subject with him," Blackwell said as the waiter returned with a glass of ice for her. As he placed martinis in front of Jennifer and me, I simply looked at Blackwell as she popped an ice cube into her mouth—and bit down hard on it. "Because if you don't talk with him about this, Lisa—and by that I mean very, very soon, like tonight or tomorrow soon—you really are screwed. Because if he wants you to be a June bride in this city, we need to start planning your wedding for *next* June, not this one."

2

———

LATER THAT NIGHT, when I returned home by cab to the brick-and-limestone townhouse Tank and I called home on Park and Seventy-Third, it was nearly ten o'clock—and I had a sinking sensation in my gut about our pending nuptials as I unlocked the front door and stepped inside the dimly lit foyer.

I shrugged off my black winter coat, removed my black leather gloves, and put both into the closet as I heard Tank coming toward me from the living room.

I knew my man. At this time of night, he was likely winding down by reading one of his thrillers. And so, when he emerged around the corner and stepped into the foyer wearing a white T-shirt, boxers, and his glasses, I knew that's exactly what he'd been doing.

"How are you?" I asked as I fell into his arms.

"Missing you," he said.

"You don't say."

"The house seems empty without you in it."

Just as my heart would be empty without you in it...

"Have you been reading?" I asked.

"I have."

"Is the book any good?"

"Not nearly as good as seeing you right now," he said, and then he reached out and held me tightly against him.

Tank's body was so fit and hard that hugging him was almost was like hugging a brick wall—not that I minded it. I loved the feeling of my cheek buried within the valley of his chest and the way his muscular arms slung low around my waist, his fingertips lightly brushing the curve of my ass. But most of all I loved how he smelled—masculine and earthy —and also how safe he made me feel when he held me like this.

"How was your night out with Jennifer and Blackwell?" he asked, leaning back and brushing a few strands of hair away from my forehead.

"Complicated."

"Complicated? I was expecting to hear that it was fun."

"It wasn't."

"Why?"

"How early do you need to get to bed tonight?"

"It's Saturday, remember? I'm off tomorrow, so if you need to talk, I'm good to talk for however long you need to talk."

"Then we probably should talk," I said.

"That doesn't sound good..."

"Have you had anything to drink tonight?"

"Just water."

"Let me get you a scotch."

"It's that bad?"

"I don't know, Tank. We'll see, I guess. Let me get us both a drink, and I'll meet you in the living room."

"See you there in a minute."

When I joined him with our drinks—a martini for me, a

tumbler of scotch for him—I saw that he had a fire roaring in the fireplace. It lit the room with a flickering orange hue. He was seated in his favorite leather wingback chair, his Kindle and a glass of water on the table next to him.

"Here," I said, giving him his drink and a kiss on the lips.

"Sit on my lap," he said as he patted his thigh.

I sat down and wrapped my free arm around his neck.

"So, what's going on?" he asked after taking a sip of his drink. "Was it something Blackwell said?"

"How did you guess?"

"Because it's rarely Jennifer. What's the problem? I have a feeling it has to do with the wedding."

"And you would be correct."

"Logistics?"

"They continue to be an issue," I said in frustration. "I've tried to involve you in as little of this as possible because I thought for sure that Jennifer, Blackwell, and I could hammer out the details while you focused on work. But it's not that simple anymore."

"What's not that simple?"

As I sipped my martini, I knew I had no choice but to just tell him the worst. "We can't get married in Manhattan."

"Because everything is still booked?"

"Yes. You know I've tried everything, but I'm afraid that when it comes to this city, you have to plan a good year or two out to get what you really want. And what I really want is to become your June bride."

"You still can be if you want to, Lisa."

"But how?" I said. "Because it sure as hell isn't happening here."

"Does it have to happen here? Because if it doesn't, I have an idea."

"What idea? I thought you wanted to get married *here*."

"What I want is to get married to *you*. In June. So, how about this? What if we got married at your parents' place?"

"I'd love to, but I couldn't do that to them," I said. "Mom and Dad's motel might be small, but it's super busy in June. I'd never want to put that kind of pressure on them."

"Then I have another idea...which you probably won't like."

"At this point, I'll take whatever ideas you have."

"We'll see about that," he said.

"It can't be that bad," I said. "Come on—this is about us! This is about finally becoming man and wife! If you have something in mind, I need to hear it, because I'm that desperate. So, tell me—what's the idea?"

"I think you need to down your martini right now, Lisa," he said.

"Excuse me?"

"Just down it. And don't worry—I'll do the same with my scotch, because I already know that both of us are going to need it."

"Are you being serious?"

"I am."

"Well, then," I said, not knowing what he was up to, "bottoms up!"

I swallowed my drink just as he tossed back his, and then I put my glass on the side table and planted the palms of my hands firmly against his chest.

"What's your plan, man?" I asked.

"First, I need to know if you really do want to get married this year."

Is he serious? Does he really have no idea how long I've waited for this?

"I do want to get married this year—as in June. As in STAT!"

"You're sure about that?"

"Tank, more than anything, I want to become your June bride. And this year, I *will* become that June bride—no matter what it takes."

"Then you might have to become my June bride in Prairie Home, Nebraska," he said. "Or *No*braska, as you like to say."

I nearly choked. "*Sorry-what-was-that-come-again?*"

"You heard me."

"Prairie Home?" I said. "Otherwise known as the land in which your mother hates me?"

"She doesn't hate you."

"The hell she doesn't."

"She doesn't. It's just that she doesn't understand why you write about zombies, that's all. She's super religious— you know that. It's confusing to her. She'd rather you wrote about kittens."

"Like *that's* going to happen."

"Here's the thing," he said, taking hold of my hands and kissing the backs of them. "We could get married on my parents' property, which is spectacular. You know they own several hundred acres. Sure, a lot of it is farmland, but around the house? I know you've only seen it in winter, but the land is amazing. If I told Mom and Dad that we wanted to get married there in June, there's plenty of time for us to build a big gazebo near the pond in the backyard, which just happens to be filled with swans."

"There are swans on the property?" I asked.

"Dozens of them. They come back every year to nest. If nothing else, they and the pond would make a romantic backdrop."

I had to admit they would, and so I did. "OK, so the

swans and the pond are a plus," I said. "As is the gazebo. Go on."

"Now that we know that Manhattan is out of the question, we have plenty of time to plan for a wedding in Prairie Home. My parents would welcome it. Plus, we have to consider that Mom is terrified of flying. We were planning to bus each of them in if we got married here. But if we got married there, we wouldn't have to do that, which would make things easier on them."

As he spoke, already I was having second thoughts. A pretty gazebo and some sleek swans could never mask the fact that his mother loathed me. I was about to speak when he looked me in the eyes.

"I need my parents to hear me say my vows to you, Lisa. It's important to me. You are the love of my life. I want my parents, my friends, and my entire family to hear what I have to say when I marry you. I want them to understand why I want to spend the rest of my life with you—and also to have a family with you. If you want to get married this June—which I also want—then this is the best way to make that happen."

I put my hand on his shoulder and kissed him when he said that, but my racing thoughts cut through me like knives.

His mother despises me, I thought. *When we were there two Christmases ago, she made it clear to me in all sorts of clever and subtle ways that I wasn't good enough for her son. Several times, she tried to embarrass me in front of him. So, what is she going to do to me if we do get married there? Humiliate me even more? That woman is as formidable as Blackwell, for God's sake—and maybe even worse, because she covers her corrosiveness with a mannered smile while Blackwell never conceals who she is. Tank's mother is cruel and deceptive. But Blackwell? Blackwell would tell you to your face to take her or leave her.*

"Prairie Home," I said, wishing I hadn't finished my martini so quickly. I looked at the empty glass sitting on the side table as if it had betrayed me. "Who would have thought...?"

"Look," Tank said. "I know you, and I also know that if you're feeling any kind of reticence, it's not about Prairie Home—it's about my mother. I get it. When we spent Christmas there, she was terrible to you."

"She was," I said. "I don't mean to sound disrespectful, Tank, but she was kind of a bitch to me. You know it. Hell, you *witnessed* it. She doesn't believe I'm good enough for you —and we both know it. And since she hasn't seen me since that Christmas, can either of us expect that she's suddenly changed her mind about me now? Of course she hasn't. And why would she? We haven't been back since, and she probably thinks *I'm* the one who's keeping you from her and your father now. I know you love her. Of course you do— she's your mother. But for me, she's always going to be the good Christian who looks down on me as the woman who writes about the undead—and not kittens—and thus should have nothing to do with her son."

"Here's what matters," he said. "*I* dig what you write. I couldn't give a shit what my mother thinks about your work. And just because we haven't been back to see my parents doesn't mean I don't talk to them every week. *Or* that they don't know how much I'm in love with you. I think I've pretty much drilled that into their heads at this point."

"You have?"

"Of course I have."

"I had no idea."

"You know I call them every Sunday. They're getting

older—I need to check in on them. So, when opportunity strikes, I tell them."

"What's their response?"

"Dad's happy for me. Mom's going to take some time."

"Isn't your judgment good enough for her?"

"Her argument is that she only had a week to get to know you."

"And to judge me. I was perfectly nice to her. My parents raised me to be polite, Tank. So, why the mistreatment?"

"I don't know. Maybe it's because she always thought I'd eventually move back home and marry this girl I used to date from Prairie Home."

And when he said that, I just looked at him.

"OK—so *that* just came out of nowhere."

"That's because I have no interest in the girl she wanted me to marry. And besides, that woman is already married to a great guy I used to be on the football team with in high school. They now have two children of their own."

"You dated her in high school?"

"Yeah. You know—as in seventeen years ago. When I was a sophomore."

"And yet your mother still holds a torch for each of you? Why? Especially after all this time?"

"Probably because Linda is a member of my mother's quilting club and they see each other every Thursday night."

"Quilting club?" I said. "*Quilting club?* Now I feel as if I'm going to hurl."

"Why?"

"*Because I can't quilt!* And because your mother is going to expect me to be able to. She's going to expect me to stitch together this huge fucking quilt for you in order to keep you warm during the winter—just like *Linda* would have done if she were still single and available."

"OK, so you need to calm down—"

"Tank, regardless what your mother thinks of me, all I can do is love you with all my heart, but that's clearly not enough when it comes to her. I mean, come on—my talents are weirdly specific. They're reserved for murdering people in print and then bringing them back to life again so they can go on to murder other people. Rinse and repeat. I'm far from being the kind of domestic goddess your mother wants for you."

"Lisa, it's going to be all right."

"But how do you know that?"

"Because I've already called my mother out on her behavior."

And where did that even come from?

"You have?"

"Of course I have."

"When?"

"About a week after we left Prairie Home."

"And you're telling me this now?"

"You know me—I like to handle things like this on my own. And when it comes to how my family treats you, I consider it a private matter that I will handle on my own. My mother got an earful from me after we last saw her."

"I had no idea..."

"Well, she did."

"And how did that go over?"

"My mother wants a relationship with me. And because she does, she heard me when I told her that if she doesn't treat you with respect, she'll be seeing a whole lot less of me. You and I skipped seeing my parents this Christmas for that reason alone. I have a feeling she gets it now. I have a feeling that when you see her again, you're going to be meeting a whole different person."

"You came on that strong?"

"I did."

"And here I thought that nothing had been said..."

"I'll always take care of you, Lisa. I hope you know that. I need you to believe me when I say that my mother won't be an issue."

"But how can you promise me that, Tank? You're not her."

"You're right," he said. "I'm not—but we'll be arriving together, and she'll know that she'll have to be on her best behavior with me there."

I hadn't considered that.

"So, we do this?" he asked. "We get married in Prairie Home?"

Where is another martini when I need one? Oh, look —nowhere.

"We do," I said. "Because I see no other choice. Tomorrow we'll call your parents and see how they feel about it."

"They'll be thrilled," he said.

Will they? I wondered. *Because I'm not so sure about that, Tank. In fact, you might need to gird your loins when we make that call.*

"I have one provision," I said.

"What's that?"

"We call by speakerphone."

"Why by speakerphone?"

"Because your mother is formidable. We both know it. We also know that if it were just the two of you on the line, she might resist this. But if she knows that both of us are on the line when you call? That's going to be a hell of a lot harder for her to achieve."

"And this is why I love you," he stated.

I gave him a kiss.

"In fact, how about if we go upstairs and I show you just how much I love you?" he suggested.

"Really?"

"Really."

Without a word and in one fell swoop, Tank swept me into his arms. He stood and kissed me on the neck, and I held on tightly as he took the stairs to our bedroom on the second floor, where he made love to me for one blissful hour.

3

WHEN I AWOKE the next morning, the memory of what I'd agreed to the night before was the first thing that slammed into my consciousness. And when it did, it was like taking a solid punch to the gut.

With no options to marry here in Manhattan, I'd agreed to marry Tank on his parents' working cow-and-chicken farm in Prairie Home, *No*braska—and how would *that* smell in the heat of June?

Worse, later today we—together—planned to call Tank's mother, Ethel, to see if she'd even agree to host the event. And God only knew how that would go over, especially since she'd always wanted her only son to marry somebody by the name of Linda—who was already married with two children.

As I lay there in bed with Tank lightly snoring beside me, I looked up at the ceiling and knew that somehow I had to win Ethel over during that call. If I could do that, perhaps none of this would be as bad as I imagined.

And so, without waking Tank, I quietly slipped out of

bed, put on a pretty red-silk robe that I knew was his favorite, and after dipping into the bathroom to run a comb through my hair and toss cold water onto my face, I snuck downstairs to make my man the breakfast he deserved.

But not before I called Jennifer.

"You agreed to do *what*?" she asked when I spilled the news to her.

"You heard me," I whispered in the living room, which was as far away from our bedroom as I could get so Tank wouldn't hear me. "And frankly, what choice did I have? Come hell or high water, I will become a June bride, Jennifer. *Tank's* June bride. So, guess what? This June, I'm officially becoming his wife."

"But what about his mother?" she asked. "You told me she treated you like shit when you first met her. Does she even know about this yet?"

"No. We plan on breaking the news to her later this morning."

"Oy," she said.

"Tell me about it. I've got to win her over, Jennifer. I've got to *make* her like me. Any advice?"

"I don't know—maybe just be yourself?"

"Didn't work the first time, so why would it work now?"

"Noted." A beat passed. "She's religious, isn't she?"

"Totally. Her rosary beads are always at the hot and ready."

"How about if you tell her you're writing a novel about the second coming?"

"Hilarious. Come on—I need something concrete."

"Lisa, I'm afraid I've got nothing."

"But you won over Blackwell, for God's sake! Of course you have something."

"*Eventually* I won her over, but it was a struggle to get there, as you know. And from what you've told me, Tank's mother sounds worse."

"She *is* worse. Blackwell just judges what you're wearing. But Ethel McCollister? She stares deep into your soul and judges *you.*"

"You know," she said, "I bet you can buy a proper soul on Amazon if you searched for it. They sell everything there."

"This isn't supposed to be funny."

"I'm just trying to lighten the mood and make you laugh, because it sounds as if you need one. But I'll be honest with you, Lisa—I can't believe you're going to allow Tank's mother, of all people, to host your wedding after the way she treated you when you first met."

"What choice do I have?"

She sighed. "Pretty much none if you want this done by June. Because I agree with you—hosting your wedding would be way too much for your parents to handle. They're barely holding it together as it is."

"Exactly. So...it's happening. In a few hours, we're going to talk to Ethel via speakerphone."

"You're doing this by speakerphone?"

"Yes—and for a reason."

"What reason?"

"Because I'm not stupid. That judgmental bitch is going to know that I'm on the line when Tank calls. Whatever she has to say about this, she's going to know that I'm listening to all of it. So, get ready to get your ass down to Prairie Home, *No*braska, in June, because this shit is happening— even if it *is* on a farm!"

"Look, Lisa, we grew up in Maine and have been to plenty of farms—we both know they can be beautiful."

"Tank said the land is particularly pretty there in the summer. He also said he'd have a gazebo built for us near a pond that's filled with swans."

"Swans?"

"Yes," I said. "And apparently a shitload of them."

"Actually, that does sound pretty," she said. "So, let me give you something to think about before I go. With the right staging and the right location—and especially if you manage to get Tank's mother in line—Prairie Home might offer you something pretty sweet, don't you think? I mean, if everything comes together in your favor, think of it—you'll be surrounded by friends, a lovely location, a gazebo, and swans in a pond. The more I think of it, this could be fabulous. And the good news is that if you settle this with Tank's parents today, then we have more than enough time to plan for something epic. Because Lord knows you've wanted that epic wedding ever since we were children."

"I do want it," I said, "if only because I don't plan on getting married again. Tank is the one for me, Jennifer. He and I are going to raise a family and grow old together. I know that in my gut."

"You have my full support when it comes to this, so if you need anything from me, just ask."

"I need you and Blackwell to help me find a dress."

"Done. Now, I wish I could continue talking, lovey, but Aiden just spit up on my shoulder and in my hair."

"You've been talking to me this entire time while you've been holding him?"

"I've been *nursing* him," she said. "And by the way, let me just welcome you to what motherhood looks like, because as much as I love my boy, when he barfs on me...it isn't pretty."

"Thanks for listening to me, Jennifer."

"Anytime. Keep me in the loop. And good luck with Ethel. Call me later in the day if you need to. But right now? Right now, Aiden just hurled yet again, and I need to go."

Before I could say anything more, the line went dead.

4

AFTER TANK AWOKE and we had breakfast, we went upstairs to his office to call his mother.

"Are you OK?" he asked, squeezing my hand. "It's just a phone call..."

It was more than that, but when I said I was fine, Tank pressed the button that put us on speakerphone, and then the sound of loud dialing rang out into the room as Tank punched a series of numbers. When the line was answered and Ethel's voice echoed into the room, my stomach tightened.

"Hello?" she said. "Mitchell, is this you?"

"Hey, Mom."

"I *knew* it was you!" she exclaimed. "I saw your name come up on the new phone you bought for your father and me. And I have to tell you that the little screen that shows me who's calling is a godsend!"

"How so?"

"For one thing, it protects me from that awful Beatrice Kaiser. You remember my telling you about her recent scandal. Her daughter had an *affair* on her husband!"

"Mom, I need to tell you that Lisa is also on the phone with us—"

"I mean, can you imagine?" Ethel interrupted, charging ahead as if she hadn't heard him. "Prairie Home is only so big, Mitchell—you know that. Only three hundred or so people live here. And yet *still* she went ahead with her sordid affair with that awful Mark Dawson when she must have known that word would eventually get out."

"But that was her daughter," Tank said. "How do her actions reflect upon Beatrice? You two have always been good friends."

"Not since her daughter's cheating went public," Ethel said. "The moment that hit, Prairie Home dropped her. Well, at least the right people did. And believe me, I've taken note of who has and who hasn't."

At that moment, I reached for a piece of paper on Tank's desk, grabbed a pen, and wrote, "How very Christian of her."

He just looked uncomfortably at me as Ethel carried on.

"Anyway, enough about her. I have to tell you that I'm still trying to figure out all of this *technology* you've recently introduced me to. Like this phone—which was tricky to use at first, but which I'm getting used to—and also the Kindle you bought me last month. You will be proud to know that your mother has finally conquered it, and that's probably because I love to read more than I like to talk on the phone. You know how much I love my cozy mysteries and Christian fiction. Those are my kinds of books—good, clean books— and not the smut so many people seem to be enjoying these days, that's for sure. I mean, my goodness! This morning I saw a book on the Amazon Top 100 called *Anaconda*! And given its lewd cover, I don't think that particular book refers to any kind of snake slithering through the Amazon!"

"So, you're liking the Kindle?" Tank asked.

"I love it!" Ethel declared. "Since your father always goes to bed before I do, I sit in the living room and read for a bit before turning in. And I have to tell you that I enjoy reading in ways that I never have before. I mean, that device is just so *easy*. I have a whole list of favorite authors at this point, and I just keep plowing through everything they've written."

She paused for a moment after she'd said that and then cleared her throat as if something were caught in it.

"I have to admit that I have seen your friend Lisa's books in the Amazon Top 100, Mitchell."

"Lisa's more than just my friend, Mom. She's my fiancée."

"Yes, yes. Right, right."

"And as I tried to tell you earlier, Lisa is on the phone with us right now."

"I'm sorry, what?"

"Before you interrupted me when you went off about Beatrice Kaiser, I tried to tell you that Lisa and I are on speakerphone. We're calling you for a reason."

"Hi, Mrs. McCollister!" I said.

"Who is that—is that Lisa?"

"It is!" I said. "How are you?"

"Well, I'm just fine, thank you. And how are you, Lisa?"

"Looking forward to spring. This winter has been the devil."

"As only you would know…"

When she said that, I just cocked my head at Tank in exasperation. "Really?" I mouthed.

He just shook his head at me before he changed the subject.

"How's Dad?" he asked.

"Is he the reason you're calling?"

"No, I just thought I'd ask about Dad. How is he?"

"Funny you should ask. He's been on such a tear today that I've been counting my rosary beads in thanks that he's out of the house. I just don't need that kind of negative energy around me, especially on the Lord's day."

"What's the issue?"

"I don't know—something to do with the plumbing at one of the barns. He barked about it for a few moments after we returned from church, but I didn't pay much attention, because whenever he goes off on one of his barn rants, I have zero interest in them."

"Did he sound stressed?" Tank asked in concern.

"Yes, he sounded stressed—and he even swore! In front of me! I haven't seen him since we got back. Let's just hope he finds Christ before he returns to the house. Otherwise, I'll have to have Father Harvey take him aside next Sunday and strongly suggest that your father go to confession."

Oh, my God, I thought as I continued to listen to her. *I'm so dead when it comes to this woman, it's not funny. She judges everything and everyone. There is no way in hell that she and I are going to come together and have a relationship with one another.*

"About our news..." Tank began.

And here we go, I thought in despair.

"What news is that?" Ethel said. "And why is there an 'our' attached to it?"

"Lisa and I have set a date."

"A date for what?"

"A date to get married."

"Oh!" she said after a moment. "Oh, my—oh, my word! Really? Well, my goodness. *Well, my God.* Why is the room spinning right now? Why do I feel as if I'm about to faint? Why are the walls suddenly turning black? After hearing that, I think I need to sit down."

"I hope that means it's because you're happy for us."

"Well, *of course* I am," she said after a long moment. "I mean, my only son is about to get married! I've been waiting for this day for years!"

"We're really excited about it," Tank said.

"I'm sure you are," she replied. "I'm sure that both of you are crippled with happiness! Especially Lisa. When is the wedding?"

"June tenth—it falls on a Saturday."

"But June is only a few months away. This is happening so soon!"

"I'm afraid that's on me," he said. "On Christmas Eve, I surprised Lisa by setting the date in a card I gave to her. I've always seen her as a June bride."

"And you're just telling me about this *now*? You've known for almost two months about this? How can it be that I'm just finding out now?"

"Because of logistics," he said. "We'll get to that in a moment."

"Well," she said, "Christmas Eve. Oh, Mitchell, with the lights and the festivities alone, it must have been so romantic!"

"I tried to make it romantic."

"And he succeeded," I said as I reached for his hand. "It was beyond romantic, Ethel."

"I'm sure it was wonderful, Lisa. You must have been thrilled."

"I was over the moon," I said. "I'm so happy."

"I can only imagine," she said. "Mitchell is quite a catch."

"I agree."

"So, this is finally happening," Tank said. "We're getting married. And we're excited. But we need help from you and Dad."

"What kind of help?"

"We can't get married in Manhattan. All of the churches and reception halls are booked. And because Lisa's parents are so busy with their motel—especially during the summer months—we were wondering if we could get married in Prairie Home at the farm. Will you and Dad host our wedding for us? Because we'd love to get married there."

"In one of the barns?"

"No, not in one of the barns. Mom, what are you thinking?"

"It was a joke, Mitchell. Your mother does have a sense of humor, you know? She's slyer than you think. And if you and Lisa would like to get married here, your father and I are all in."

"Well, thanks, Mom."

"Anything for you, Mitchell."

"If it's OK with you and Dad, I'd like to build a gazebo next to the pond. Lisa and I will get married there, with the pond and the swans as a backdrop. What do you think?"

"Actually, I think that sounds *divine*," she said. "Go ahead and draw up the plans. I mean, my goodness! Lisa and you getting married at your family home! Your father is going to be beyond surprised—as I am right now! Now listen, Lisa... are you there?"

"I'm here!" I said.

"Good, because I expect to be involved in *absolutely everything*! I want to help you pick out your dress and the flowers. We need to go over the dinner menu for the reception dinner. And all sorts of other things...*because I want to be involved!* What do you think?"

How much do you want to be involved? I thought. *Fuck my life!*

"I would love your input, Mrs. McCollister," I said. "Thank you."

"Best to call me Ethel now that you're about to marry my only child. Or you can call me Mother if you want. How about that?"

You seriously want me to call you Mother? I thought. *And what the hell am I to say to that? If I say no, I'll only offend her. And since she's stepping up to the plate when it comes to this, she's pretty much cornered me!*

Tank was scribbling on a piece of paper. "You don't have to," he wrote. "Don't do it if you don't want to."

I didn't want to, but I nevertheless took one for the team.

"I'd be delighted to call you Mother," I said to Ethel. "It would be an honor. Thank you!"

"Thank you...who?"

"Thank you...Mother?"

"That has such a nice ring to it!" she said. "Oh, Lisa, I do hope we can come to know one another and be good friends. I'd really like that. I really would."

"I'd like the same," I said. "Tank means the world to me. I'd like to be close to both you and Mr. McCollister."

"Think of him as Daddy from now on. As Tank can tell you, his father always wanted a little girl to spoil. And if I didn't have a lazy ovary, he probably would have had one."

A lazy ovary? Daddy? Jesus Christ! This is going straight into some kind of bizzaro world.

Still, I knew that I had no choice but to cave.

"Daddy it is!" I said as Tank squeezed my knee in a show of support.

"Perfect—he'll love it. Now, I'm assuming this is going to be a big Catholic wedding? Because we are a Catholic family, Lisa..."

I was a lapsed Catholic and really wanted just a simple ceremony, which Tank knew.

"We have something simpler in mind, Mom," Tank said. "Nothing too long or too grand, especially given how hot it's going to be there in June. But it would be nice if Father Harvey officiated."

"Are you saying this won't be a full Catholic wedding?" she asked. "You know, with all the classic rituals? The praying? The service? The whole lot of it?"

"I am saying that."

"But I always dreamed of you having a proper wedding," she said.

"And Lisa and I plan to have that wedding—on our terms."

"I see," she said. "Well, I won't mask my disappointment, but at least a confirmed priest will be there, so there's that, I guess."

"There is that," Tank said in a firm voice.

"When am I going to get more details?" she asked. "Because I cannot wait to tell your father, Mitchell. He's especially going to want to know about that gazebo of yours."

"I'm going to have an architect draw up plans, and I'll submit them to Dad and to you as soon as I have them. I want you to love the structure as much as we do."

"As you should," she said. "I'll let your father know about that. But as for coordinating things, I assume that Lisa and I will have weekly chats to brainstorm about all of it. Is that right, Lisa?"

"I'll call you every Saturday," I said. "Because I'd hate to interrupt your Sundays, especially with church and all."

"How very sensitive of you. I'll expect a call from you at noon my time on every Saturday going forward."

"Done."

For a moment, there was a long silence. I looked at Tank, wondering if the line had gone dead, but then Ethel said, "All of this is just so sudden."

"I'm sorry about that, Mom," Tank said. "I should have planned better."

"No, no—it's fine because I'm *limber*. But as I'm trying to wrap my head around all of this, I think both of you should come down a week before the wedding. I mean, since there are going to be so many details to nail down in person, both of you need to be here sooner rather than later. Can I count on that?"

Jennifer and Alex will give you another week off, I wrote down on a piece of paper.

"We can do that, Mom," Tank said. "We'll fly out a week before the wedding."

"Then I guess that's it," she said. "And congratulations to both of you! When Harold returns from the barn, I'll tell him everything. Lisa, as you search for dresses, please send photos so we can discuss what's best. Sound good?"

"It sounds perfect," I lied.

"Then we'll talk soon. Kisses to you both! I now have news that will triumph over Beatrice Kaiser's daughter's affair with that horrible Mark Dawson person—and I plan to run with it. All of Prairie Home is going to want to come —but only a select few will be invited, because I already know this is going to be an exclusive affair, and I can't wait to be part of all of it. I want to roll up my sleeves, get my hands dirty, and tinker into everything as the months pass before the big day. And Lisa?" she said.

"Yes, Ethel?"

"Yes, Mother," she corrected.

I rolled my eyes and decided to just go with it. "Yes, Mother?"

"Wait until you see just how well I tinker..."

FOUR MONTHS LATER

5

New York City
June

On the morning of June 3, just seven days before I was to marry Tank, I put my makeup bag inside one of my suitcases, looked over everything before I closed it shut and locked it, and then stood next to Tank as he lifted it off the bed and placed it alongside the other two suitcases that were already packed and ready to go.

"Are you OK?" he asked me.

"I'm fine," I said, reaching up to kiss him. "I promise."

"I'm sorry I'm not able to come. I'm sorry you have to spend five days alone with my parents before I arrive."

"One of your best friends just died, Tank—a man you once served next to in war. And Brian died from a blood clot, of all things, and at so young an age. We've already talked about this. As far as I'm concerned, this is settled. Because it would make no sense for you to fly with me to

Prairie Home when you'd have to turn around three days
later and fly to San Diego to spend a day with his wife, children, and family before you went to his funeral the next day.
I will handle the final details of our wedding with your
mother before you fly to Nebraska on the eighth. It's not
going to be an issue, especially since your mother and I
appear to be getting along lately."

"That's not entirely true," he said, "and you know it.
She's asked a lot of you. She hasn't exactly been easy."

"It's only because she wants our wedding to be as perfect
as it can be. Now, look—you'll arrive on the eighth, your
mother and I will pick you up at the airport that day, and
then we'll return to Prairie Home together. It's all planned.
The next day, our friends will arrive for the rehearsal and
the rehearsal dinner. On Saturday, everything will be in
order, and we'll get married. I want to make this as easy on
you as possible. You deserve that from me, especially given
the weight of your loss. I only wish that I'd met Brian—
that's my regret. It sounds like he was a wonderful man,
Tank. I'm so sorry that you lost your friend."

"So am I." He took me into his arms and held me for a
long moment. "You're an amazing woman, Lisa Ward."

"Soon to be Lisa McCollister," I said in his ear. And
when I said that, with my cheek pressed against his, I felt
him smile—which was all I needed to know that I was doing
the right thing despite the uncertainty I felt.

Was I nervous about the prospect of spending five days
alone with Tank's mother? Hell, yes. But during my talks
with his father on the phone over the past several months,
Harold had been nothing but genuinely kind to me, so I
knew in my gut that I had nothing to worry about when it
came to him. But Ethel and me? We had a checkered past.
As good as she'd been to me over these past several months

—literally going out of her way in many cases to make certain our wedding would go off without a hitch—we'd also had our share of issues, from the dress I'd chosen (too revealing, according to her) to what the caterer would be serving ("Here in Prairie Home, I guess we're not as fancy as you are in Manhattan").

But for the most part—and if I were being honest—this wedding meant a lot to her. Tank was her only child, and as God was my witness, this would be his only wedding. So, on those days when she was difficult, I got it. She wanted to have her say, and that came with its share of bumps.

As for my parents? They were a breeze. Unlike Jennifer's parents, who were risible people I'd like to smother in their sleep, my parents were phenomenal. My mother loved the dress I chose with the help of Jennifer and Blackwell, and both my parents were fully onboard when it came to my marrying Tank, whom they'd adored when we visited them for the first time as a couple in March. They had offered to pay for the wedding, and they'd been gracious enough to do so even though I wasn't getting married in my home state. But since I knew that the financial strain was just too much for them to bear at this point in their lives, I'd gently let them off the hook.

My parents were just chill, cool people who typically rolled with whatever was tossed their way. There was no drama when it came to my mama, and since I'd included her in everything along the way, I knew she also felt vested in this and that my father felt the same.

"I should go," I said. "Jennifer will be here to pick me up soon."

"I wish you'd let me drive you."

"I can't do airport goodbyes," I said. "If you drove me to LaGuardia, and the last thing I saw was your face, I'd just be a wreck. Hell, I'm going to need that drive to the airport just to have Jennifer talk me off a cliff about leaving you alone like this. Trust me—this is the best way."

"I get it," he said. "I'm going to miss you, Lisa."

"And I'm going to miss you, Tank. I really am. But in a few days, all this will be behind us, and we'll be man and wife."

My cell rang as I said that, and I knew it would be Jennifer. As I removed my phone from my pants pocket, I checked the display. Sure enough, it was Jennifer.

"Hello?" I said.

"It's me, sweetcakes. Are you ready to do this? Because I'm double-parked outside your front door—and traffic won't be very happy with me if you don't move it along."

"On it!" I said. "See you in seconds."

I clicked off my phone, put it in my pocket, and looked at Tank. "Jennifer's outside," I said. "We should hurry before people start honking their horns at her for clogging the street."

Before I left for good, Tank swept me into his arms with such passion and meaning that I literally felt his heart pounding against mine as he held me close to him while he kissed me on the neck, cheek, and lips. He told me that he loved me. He thanked me for doing this without him. And then I told him I would do anything for him—absolutely anything. Because our love for each other deserved that. It was something to be respected—and I refused to allow anyone or anything to break it.

WHEN I LEFT OUR TOWNHOUSE, I was relieved to see that traffic was able to maneuver around Jennifer's limousine—

nobody was blowing their horns at her. All seemed to be good when Cutter sprang out of the car, said hello to me, and joined Tank in getting all my bags into the limo's trunk.

"So, this is it for now," I said to Tank as I felt the warmth of the bright sunshine on my shoulders. "Give me a kiss."

When he did, it was so charged with his love for me that I just drank all of it in as we stood there on the sidewalk while a flood of people hurried past us in an effort to get to work. It was seven in the morning, and Manhattan was coming alive.

"I'll see you before you know it," he said to me.

"I'm counting on that."

"But in the meantime, I'm going to miss the hell out of you, Lisa."

"We're doing the right thing," I promised him. And I meant it, because I knew that if he didn't go to his friend's funeral, he'd regret it—which I just couldn't have. "Please remember me to Brian's wife and family. I know we haven't met, but I want them to know that I will be with them in spirit."

"I'll make sure they know that," he said.

I looked over at the car as Cutter swung open the back door for me. And when he did, a wealth of emotions overcame me. Tank and I were parting now, and I couldn't help the tears that brightened my eyes.

"I should go," I said. "And soon—before I start to cry."

"I'll see you soon," he said.

"Very soon. I love you, Tank. Please know that I'll always be with you."

And with a surprising depth of emotion in his voice, Tank—who rarely revealed his emotions to anyone—nevertheless shared his with me now. "You are the single best thing that has ever happened to me in my life. I need you to know that."

"I do know it," I said to him. "Because you show it to me every day. But I need to go—I'll break if I don't."

And so, with a final kiss on his lips, I stepped inside the car—and as I did, the hand that reached out to help me wasn't Jennifer's.

Instead, it was Blackwell's.

6

"WELL," Blackwell said as Cutter shut the door behind me. "That couldn't have been easy. I mean, just look at Tank, for God's sake. Look at his face. If that isn't the look of pure love, I don't know what is."

She checked me when she said that, and her hand immediately dipped inside her purse to remove a Kleenex from it as I sat beside her and opposite Jennifer, who was looking at me with concern.

"Here," Blackwell said, handing me the tissue. "I know this is hard on both of you. Take it, my dear. Use it. Because it appears as if you might need to."

"Thank you," I said, dabbing the tissue beneath my eyes as Cutter got into the front seat and cut out into traffic. I looked over my shoulder and saw Tank a final time. He was standing on the sidewalk with his right hand raised high in the air as he waved goodbye to me. And just seeing him like that—alone with the burden of having to go to his friend's funeral during the very week of our wedding—cut through me to the point that tears welled in my eyes.

"I'm sorry," I said as Tank faded from sight. "I'm usually tougher than this."

"Being tough is a virtue," Blackwell said. "I'll be the first to champion that. But being human also is one. Never forget that, Lisa. The love Jennifer and I just witnessed between you and Tank is the very reason you are getting married to him. And him to you."

When Jennifer leaned forward and put her hand on my knee, I knew that she, like Blackwell, felt my pain—and then I just took a deep breath in an effort to collect myself. I rarely cried in front of anyone. In fact, I *hated* to cry in front of anyone. It's just not how I rolled.

"My apologies," I said as I pulled myself together.

"Lisa, you are under so much stress, why *wouldn't* you be upset that Tank isn't with you now?" Jennifer asked. "I brought Blackwell with me for a reason—because if anyone can say the right words to you, it's her."

I looked over at Blackwell, who wore a bright-yellow Chanel suit with matching heels, and I took the hand she proffered.

"Thank you for coming," I said. "I didn't know you'd be here. I thought you'd be at work now."

"I've already been to Wenn," she said. "Jennifer and I had this planned the moment we learned that Tank needed to go to his friend's funeral. Right now at Wenn, people think I'm just at some random meeting that will last for *hours.* So, don't worry about me. We're good. I'm where I should be."

"Thank you for taking care of me," I said to each of them. "Because I'm not going to lie—that was hard as hell. I should be going to that funeral with him, and yet I'm not."

"Tank needs to support his friend," Blackwell said. "And he also needs to spend time with Brian's family. Meanwhile, you have your wedding to prepare for, which is also important. The timing is unfortunate, Lisa, but it is what it is—and both of you are doing the right thing."

"Why don't we put all of this behind us and look to next week?" Jennifer suggested. "Because Barbara and I think you might need some guidance when it comes to being alone with Tank's mother, and we wanted to share a few tips before you landed there later today."

"What tips?" I asked.

"Before we begin with them, you aren't traveling first class as you thought you were," Jennifer said. "Instead, you are taking one of Wenn's private jets."

"I'm flying on Wenn's private what?" I asked.

"You heard me," she said. "Just think of it as one of your wedding gifts."

"But why?" I asked.

"Because right now, you deserve to fly private," Blackwell said. "You deserve to be alone with your thoughts before you have to deal with Tank's mother."

"But what does that mean? She's been pretty nice to me lately. And I know she's excited about the wedding."

"I understand that she's come around, but Jennifer and I had a discussion on the drive over here, and we each believe you should have your guard up when it comes to her."

"I don't understand."

"For months she's thought that her son would be arriving with you," Blackwell said. "The fact that he isn't is a game changer. Soon she'll have you to herself, and don't think she doesn't know it. Never forget that a leopard can hide in plain sight, Lisa, and that it never changes its spots. You need to pay close attention to how that little Holy Roller treats you without Tank there to protect you."

"This is all I need to hear," I said.

"We could be wrong," Blackwell said. "And let's hope we are. But since you never know, we wanted you to be fully armed for anything."

"Speaking of Ethel," I said, "she thinks I'm coming in on a United flight. Since I'm now apparently flying private, what do I tell her? Because I've got to text her something. And when she first hears of this, she's going to think I'm being pretentious."

"Let her think what she wants," Blackwell said. "Text her that you've changed your mind about United and that you've decided to fly private. Say nothing more, because the other message you're sending her is already implied."

"What other message?"

"That you are *able* to fly private. From everything you've told me about her, Ethel McCollister doesn't understand just how successful you are, or—worse—that she doesn't *want* to understand. Either way, your arriving in a private jet might change her perspective of you. Because if that doesn't impress her, Lisa, I'm not sure what will."

"I'm not out to impress her, Barbara."

"Then you're a fool when it comes to that one. Because when you tell her that you've decided to fly private, she's going to see you with new eyes. Eyes that hopefully will have a measure of respect in them."

"I know her better than that. She's only going see this as a gaudy show of money."

"Oh, my dear," Blackwell said. "Never, ever underestimate the power of money. Because money always talks, and money has the power to influence others into silence. I say you dazzle this new 'mother' of yours when you walk off that jet." She turned to Jennifer. "Where and when will Lisa be arriving?"

"When she was on United, she was landing around four.

But with us, she's landing at three."

"So, are we doing this?" Blackwell said.

I thought about it for a moment, finally deciding that Blackwell was right once again. I should go into Prairie Home with a sense of confidence at my back. And this would help.

"I'll do it," I said. "But if I am going to do it, I'm not going to pretend I paid for this on my own. I don't lie. So I expect Jennifer to bill me. No arguments."

"Lisa, that isn't necessary," Jennifer said.

"I won't do it otherwise," I said. "And I mean it."

"All right," she said with a sigh. "And actually, I see your point. You don't want to feel like a fraud if she questions you about it."

"Exactly. So, you'll bill me?"

"I don't want to, but I will."

"I have to text her about the changes," I said, removing my SlimPhone from my handbag and switching it on. "Where is she going to pick me up? She'll need to know."

Jennifer told me.

"She's so going to judge me when it comes to this," I said as I started to tap out the text.

"Or revere you for it," Blackwell said. "Lisa, Ethel McCollister might indeed privately resent you for flying in on a massively expensive Learjet, but from what you've told me about her, I think she'll brag to her friends about it. Do you think I'm wrong?"

"When you put it that way? Not at all."

"Then hit send."

I sent the text.

"Now, let's get you on that plane."

～

WHEN WE WERE at LaGuardia and it was time to say goodbye to Jennifer and Blackwell, I heard my phone ding in my handbag.

"She just texted me back," I said.

"What did she say?" Jennifer asked as I removed my cell from my handbag and read the message.

"Just as I expected," I said. "Shall I read it?"

"Please do," Blackwell said.

"'You're flying private?'" I read. "'Well, my goodness, Lisa, there's no need to fly private here—trust me, because there's nobody here to impress. I mean, certainly not me. You can just be yourself here, and I hope that you will be. Nevertheless, I'll still be waiting for you at the designated location. I will see you soon. Best, Mother.'" I looked at them both. "Saying 'best' is the worst. She already hates me again."

"Actually, with this knowledge," Blackwell said, "she's rethinking everything when it comes to you."

"What do you mean?"

"That if she didn't understand it before, she now knows that you truly are a woman of means, that you won't compromise your life for anyone, and that she underestimated you. Because of that, you'll never become her pawn. Of course, she can try to turn you into one if she wants, and she might. But on some level, she must know now that achieving that goal just came with a very steep incline that even our dear Ethel didn't see coming."

TWENTY MINUTES LATER, after saying my goodbyes, I was seated on the exquisitely designed jet and sipping a strong Bloody Mary before we took off for the five-hour trip to Prairie Home—where God only knew what awaited me.

7

WHAT AWAITED me once I got off the plane, crossed the hot tarmac, and entered the FBO hangar—which all private aircraft had to use instead of one of the airport's gates—was Ethel McCollister herself. When I first laid eyes on her as I entered the small lounge, I saw again where Tank had gotten his good looks.

When she was young, Ethel must have been stunning, because in the fall of her life, she was beautiful.

"Lisa," she said, rising and holding out her arms to me. "Come and let me have a good look at you. It's been so long!"

Ethel was a tall reed of a woman somewhere in her early sixties, although due to good genes, she looked years younger. She had a coiffed helmet of blond hair, her face was lightly tanned and had a healthy glow about it, her lips were painted deep red, and she was dressed completely in white—stylish slacks, a fitted blazer buttoned once at the waist, and a camisole that betrayed not one millimeter of cleavage.

If she were sitting on a cloud right then, she might be mistaken for an angel, which probably was her intent.

But what nearly stopped me in my tracks was that hanging from her right shoulder to her left hip was a gorgeous Double V Louis Vuitton handbag in beige, which I knew for a fact had set her back four grand. Even though I knew the McCollisters were successful, Tank and I had never once discussed just how successful. Right now, that handbag of hers was doubling down in an effort to let me know that the McCollisters had money.

Really? I thought as I walked toward her with a smile. *You judged me for flying private and yet you're carrying* that *bag? Who's trying to impress whom, Ethel?*

Whenever I flew, I dressed comfortably. Today, that had meant a pair of black Dolce & Gabbana midrise skinny cropped pants and a white scoop-necked tank by Givenchy. On my feet were a pair of black Christian Louboutin T-strap sandals with a red sole. My handbag was a black city satchel bag by Prada. I was dressed more casually than Ethel, but I was still working it—and thank God I was, because as I reached out to give Ethel a hug, I saw her assess me in one swift, calculated glance.

"It's good to see you," I said in her ear. "Thank you again for all your hard work and help. And for allowing us to host our wedding here."

"It's our pleasure," she said as she took a step back to soak me in. "You look trim and terrific, Lisa. You really do."

"And I can only say the same thing to you," I said, meaning it. "Not only is that suit of yours on point, but I'm blown away by your bag. It's gorgeous."

"I bought it in the city last week," she said. "I went on a rare shopping spree. The bag, of course, is a treat for my son's wedding, and I simply adore it, even if Harold nearly collapsed when he saw how much it cost. But since our son is only going to get married once, I think I'm off the hook. I also bought outfits for the rehearsal, the rehearsal dinner, and the wedding itself. I'll show them to you later, after you've settled in, because I'd love your opinions on each of them. You always look so chic, Lisa—and not in a sluttish, city kind of way, because I don't mean that *at all*."

Did she just throw shade at me?

I couldn't be sure, so I just carried on.

"Thank you," I said.

"Ms. Ward," said a voice behind me. I turned and saw a young man standing in the doorway with my carryon and three bags sitting on a small trolley. "Do you have a car nearby?"

"Yes, yes," Ethel said. "Just outside, in the designated parking area. It's the black Lincoln Navigator." She looked at me. "I knew you'd be bringing a slew of bags with you, so I brought the beast with me. You'll love it—it drives like a charm, although it's so huge, I have to admit it's sometimes difficult to see out the side mirrors, which scares the dickens out of me—and it might out of you, too! So, how about if we go? Because I have big plans for tonight, and Prairie Home awaits!"

AFTER MY BAGS were packed into the back, I walked around to the passenger door, remembering with a sense of relief that the drive to Prairie Home was relatively short. Depending on traffic, the McCollisters' home was about a thirty-minute drive away, which was perfect, because Ethel loved to talk.

When I opened my door, I was about to step inside

when I saw several books stacked on my seat, a mix of two hardcover novels and another in paperback—and in one horrific glance, I saw they were mine. They'd been placed there on purpose. I'd been meant to see them.

But why?

"Oh!" she said as she got inside and shut her door. "Sorry! I should have put those in the back seat."

"You bought my books?" I asked her.

"In fact, I did! I stopped at Barnes & Noble on the way over and scooped them up so I could read them over the next week. I wanted to get all of them in hardcover, but your first one is out of print at this point, so I got the trade-paper-back version instead. I know I should have read them sooner, and I apologize for not doing so because the covers frighten the devil out of me, but I am resolved to read them while you are here, Lisa. And I'm such a fast reader, I'll have them read in no time. And then we can sit down and discuss them!" She pointed a finger at me. "I'm doing this because I want to see what's in that head of yours. If you are going to marry my son and become my daughter-in-law, I want to know what you're capable of. You know, when it comes to your craft. What do you think of that?"

That I want to puke at the very idea of what those conversa-tions are going to be like, Ethel? That I have a feeling you'll be reading them with your rosary beads clutched close to your chest? That you'll wake me up in the morning by splashing holy water on my face?

"I'm honored," I said as she started the car and turned on the air conditioning.

"As you know, I've never read anything in this genre, but I certainly can give it a chance, can't I? Especially since they are *your* books. And look at me! I didn't even buy them on my Kindle, because one day I might want to showcase them in our library."

One day? Might?

"Physical books are special," she said. "They can last an eternity. Now, here," she said, moving the books to the back seat. "Sit down, buckle up, and relax. I can only imagine how exhausted you must be after that private flight of yours, which must have been strenuous. Why don't you rest while we listen to something special on the drive to Prairie Home?"

"What's that?" I asked as I took my seat and shut the door behind me.

"I've been listening to a series of spellbinding audio-books, and there's one series in particular that I'm coming to absolutely *adore*. I know you aren't religious, Lisa, so forgive me, because this series of books is very religious. It's not my intention to bore you with the teachings of the church, so think of it this way—when you start to listen and if you feel bored, just sleep."

"It's not that I'm not religious," I said, "because I do believe in God—very much so. I hope you know that."

"Actually, I didn't."

"Well, I do."

"And what a relief to hear. Do you mind if we talk a little bit about this? Because the church is very near and dear to me, Lisa. I'm sure Mitchell has told you so."

At some point, we're going to have this talk anyway, Ethel, so it might as well be now.

"We can talk about anything you'd like."

"Do you go to church?"

"I haven't been to a church in years."

"And yet you still believe in God?"

"Not going to church hasn't stolen away my faith. I'm a very spiritual person."

"Spiritual or religious?"

"I don't see a difference. For me, believing in God is believing in God."

"How very interesting. Did your parents take you to church as a child?"

"For several years they did. But that eventually stopped when my parents purchased a small motel in Bangor. Since they were financially strapped at the time and couldn't afford to hire maids, it was just the three of us left to maintain the motel, which was difficult. There was the main building to clean, which had nine rooms. And then there were ten cottages that stretched to the right of it, some of which were outfitted with full living rooms and kitchens. The three of us needed to clean all of them quickly so that we could rent them again."

"So, your reasons for not going to church came down to work?"

"As it does for many people, Ethel."

"How old were you when you stopped going to service?"

"Around nine, I think."

"My word," she said, her eyes widening at me. "So young..."

"My parents did their best. It wasn't an easy life."

"That I can fully understand. I mean, imagine how difficult it was for us with the farm, especially with so many chickens and cows to care for. As you know, back then there also was just the three of us, but we still managed to take an hour or so out of our hectic lives every Sunday to go to church. Sometimes I don't know how we did it, but we did. Likely because of God's good graces. It's a shame your parents couldn't have found just a slice of time to take themselves and you."

"Sundays followed the busiest night of the week for us," I said with a slight edge to my voice. "It also was the day all the lawns needed to be mowed, which I had to do. There was no time for church."

"I hope you don't think that I'm judging you," she said.

"I also hope you aren't, Ethel."

"That's twice you've called me by my first name, you know?"

"I do know."

"Oh, I hope that I haven't upset you with all of this church talk. It's just that I want to get to know you, Lisa...to understand you better, because I really do want for that to happen, especially since I'm about to be part of your life for the rest of my life. It's one of the reasons I'm going to read your books while you're here. You and I barely know each other, and yet in a week, you're marrying my only child. It's important for me to get to know my future daughter-in-law, and what better way to do that than through conversation?"

"I understand," I said. "And I'm sure we'll do plenty of talking over the next week."

"We should go," she said. "But first let me show you what we'll be listening to. I haven't started it yet, but I'm dying to."

She leaned forward and removed a CD case from the Navigator's glove box.

"Here, have a look," she said as she gave it to me.

The first thing I saw was the title: *Former Satanist Becomes Catholic.* The second thing I noted was the image of a priest wielding a large crucifix beneath the title as if warding off Lucifer himself. Stunned that she'd dare give this to me after that little chat, I turned the CD over and read the book's description:

How GREAT a threat is the occult? In this provocative testimony, former Satanist Betty Brennan shares the story of her remarkable journey from a dark existence of devil worship to the fulfillment of truth in Jesus Christ and the Catholic Church. You will be enlightened by her amazing sojourn, her search for deliverance, and her mission to open the eyes of others to the truth of the devil.

First the books, then the talk, and now this? She's totally setting me up to see how I'll react.

And so I reacted.

"'The truth of the devil,'" I said, returning the CD to her with a smile. "You know, I think I do need to listen to something exactly like this right now. Thank you for suggesting it."

"My pleasure," she said as she slipped the disc into the CD player and then patted me on the knee. "Let's share this experience together, Lisa. Let's hear Betty tell us about the devil and how it reveals itself in all its many forms. And if you'd like, later we can pray. Or not. Whatever you wish. Now, let's go. I promised Harold that you and I would cook dinner together tonight, because if you're going to be cooking for our son, I'm dying to see your skills at work in the kitchen."

And the hits just keep on coming.

"What will we be cooking?" I asked her.

"Why, Mitchell's favorite meal, of course," she said. "Certainly you know what that is by now. And let me tell you this, my darling girl—Mother can't wait to see how well you pull it off!"

8

HALF AN HOUR LATER, after driving out of the city and into the lush Nebraska countryside—parts of which reminded me of my home in Iowa, which made me long for it—we were nearing the McCollister home just as Betty Brennan pronounced through the Navigator's speakers that's she'd eventually found the courage to smite the devil from her life and allow God into it.

"Wasn't that inspiring?" Ethel gushed as she turned off the stereo.

"Completely," I said, looking out my window at acres upon acres of beautiful farmland. And then, only because I knew she'd made me listen to that shit on purpose, I couldn't help but go further than I otherwise would have. "Should I ever need to, I now know how to smite the devil."

"Consider it fodder for an upcoming book. I thought it was fabulous."

"Didn't you think it was even a little bit over the top?" I asked.

"Not at all. We were just listening to a former Satanist

who literally went through hell in an effort to find God. That couldn't have been easy."

"Well, it certainly didn't sound easy, because if nothing else, Betty sure did deliver her story with bravado. For a moment there, I thought she was going to lose her voice, particularly when she channeled her version of the devil. Now, *that* part was arresting. I even heard you try to stifle a laugh when she started to squeal like a pig."

"If I was doing anything, I was choking back tears."

Oh, come on, I thought. *Seriously? Lady, give me some hope for our relationship—whatever that looks like after the shit you've pulled on me today. Jennifer and Blackwell were right—I needed to come armed for anything. Thank God they made sure I wasn't too comfortable with you.*

"Anyway," she said, "we're here."

When I turned to look at the McCollister property, it was nothing like I remembered it.

The last time I'd seen the house and the surrounding grounds, they'd been masked by mounds of snow. But now, in the middle of June, the grass was such a preternatural green that it seemed lit from within. And then there were the gardens surrounding the house, which were in full bloom and popping with a host of vibrant colors. Most I recognized as established perennials—butterfly weed, Virginia bluebells, hardy geraniums, and aromatic asters— but a few urns held some lovely annuals that would bloom all summer long.

The house itself was a massive turn-of-the-century colonial with three dormers that stretched along the expansive roof. Painted bright white with black shutters, it had what appeared to be more than a dozen windows facing the circular gravel driveway, which led to a covered front porch supported by six pillars. As Ethel swung in at the front of the house, I noted the lovely portico, which she drove under to park the SUV.

"Your home is stunning," I said to her. "The last time I saw it, there were no details—just so much snow. It's amazing."

"Well, thank you, Lisa. I rather like it myself. Harold and I had the house freshened with new paint last year, so consider yourself lucky, because now it looks especially nice. I've never had a wedding on these grounds, but there have been plenty of church events and social gatherings, which is one of the main reasons we are so diligent in its upkeep."

"Tank told me the house was built in the early nineteenth century, but it looks so new," I said. "You've taken impeccable care of it. And look at the grounds over there. Is that the meadow Tank was referring to?"

"It is, and the pond and the new gazebo are off to the right, too far away to see from here. I'll show them to you later, after we say hello to Harold, who I know is anxious to see you." She opened her door and stepped out, but not before I heard her say, "The question is whether he's working in one of the barns or he's in the house."

I opened my door, stretched when I got out, and then watched as Ethel came around the car with her cell held to her ear.

"We're here," she said in a bright voice. "Where are you? In the kitchen? We'll be right in. No, you stay there. Call one of the farmhands and ask them to bring Lisa's suitcases into the house. There's no need for you to do it—you'd probably throw out your back if you even tried. I mean, my goodness —Lisa brought three bags with her *and* a carryon." She winked at me when she said, "When I first saw how much she'd packed, she gave me a little fright, because for a moment I thought she was planning to move in with us. Right, right. We'll see you in seconds."

She switched off her phone, tossed it into her Louis, and motioned to the black door at the side of the house. "Shall we?" she said, opening it. "I hate to keep Harold waiting, which is just one of the many reasons we've been married over forty years now. Never keep the man of the house waiting, Lisa. You'll do well to listen to me when it comes to that. The kitchen, you might remember, is through the mudroom and straight down the center hallway. Now, come on, after you—because Daddy wants to see you."

WHEN I ENTERED THE LARGE, sunny kitchen with its pale-yellow walls, white woodwork, golden oak floors, and professional-grade stainless-steal appliances, Harold McCollister—a tall man around his wife's age but who looked older, likely because life on the farm wasn't an easy life for anybody—gave me a smile I knew in my heart was genuine.

Tank might have inherited his mother's good looks, but he had also inherited his father's kindness of spirit. Over the last four months, I'd spoken to him often on the phone about the wedding, and with each conversation, I could feel a bond starting to build between us. I bet that irritated Ethel to no end.

"Lisa," he said as he came over to shake my hand. "It's great to see you."

"Thank you...Daddy," I said, cringing that I'd even agreed to call him something a six-year-old would call her father. "It's great to see you, too."

I'm an adult, I thought as we shook hands and he looked

at me with questioning eyes. *Why did I ever allow her to press me into calling them Mother and Daddy? Just in the hope that things would go smoothly between us? Apparently. I should have listened to Tank when he'd said I didn't need to do it. But, whatever. What's done is done.*

"Daddy?" he said, sounding surprised. He must have caught the discomfort on my face, because he turned to his wife, who was standing at my left. "You put her up to this, didn't you, Ethel?"

"Whatever do you mean?"

"Since when does Lisa call me Daddy? What is she calling you? Mommy?"

"Actually, I went for Mother," Ethel said. "Lisa is about to become our daughter-in-law, Harold. I want her to think of us as part of a family now, especially since she will officially be a McCollister in a matter of days."

"And she was too polite to turn you down." He looked at me. "Never mind about all that. I'll always be Harold to you, Lisa. And Ethel will be Ethel. So, now that that's settled, that's the end of it. How was your trip?"

"She flew private," Ethel said before I could speak. "Nothing but luxury for that one."

Bitch, please.

"Private?" he said. "That must have been nice. Good for you. What kind of plane was it?"

"I think it was a Learjet."

"It's not yours?"

"No, no—I rented it."

"You work hard," he said, "and you're successful. Why not spoil yourself a bit before your wedding? I'm sure that's the reason for the splurge, and I bet it was relaxing."

"It was something," I said, wanting to change the subject. "How have you been, Harold?"

"Same as I was when I saw you two Christmases ago, Lisa—happy and healthy, which are the two things that matter most. Other than that, my life is pretty much routine. Nothing really changes here, except when something goes haywire in one of the barns. I think the only difference you might have noticed is that my hair is starting to go from gray to white."

"It suits you," I said. "Now your eyes look bluer than Tank's, which is saying something."

"I suppose it is," he said with a smile. "So, tell me, are you working on a new book?"

"I just finished one—it's with my editor now. I'll start the new one after Tank and I return from our honeymoon."

"What's the name of the one you finished?"

Oh, dear God, please don't let me have to tell them the title...

"*I'd* certainly like to hear the title," Ethel said.

I'll bet you would, Ethel. So, fine—let me just spell it out for you.

"It's called *The Dead Will Rise*," I said.

Beside me, Ethel actually stiffened before she genuflected.

"Quit it with the showbiz, Ethel," Harold said.

"I don't know what you're talking about, Harold."

He leveled her with a look before he turned to me. "Catchy title," he said. "I bet it'll go to number one, just like the rest of them have. And you know what, Lisa? It's going to be good to have a writer in the family."

"Thank you," I said. "I appreciate that."

"Speaking of that," Ethel said. "I stopped at a bookstore on the way to the airport, and I bought all of her books! They're in the back seat of the Navigator. I plan on reading every one of them before the wedding. You know, so I can get to know Lisa better. Come to understand how her mind works and all that."

"She's not a lab experiment, Ethel."

"I never said she was, Harold."

"Lisa is a writer."

"*Well, of course she is.*"

"And she writes *fiction.*"

"I fully understand that." She gawked at him. "My good-ness—*you're* awfully feisty this afternoon."

"Just doing the Lord's work," he said. And when he said that, Harold McCollister smiled at me.

"You know," Ethel said after clearing her throat, "Lisa and I are going to cook for you tonight."

"Tonight?" he said. "But Lisa just traveled hours to be with us. She probably wants to get settled in and have *you* cook for *her*. And besides, I know for a fact that she's likely eager to see the gazebo in person, not just in the photographs we've sent. And also the pond and the swans. Why do you want her to cook?"

"Because I thought it would be fun for us. I mean, she hasn't exactly had a *grueling* day. She did fly private, after all. I thought she'd be *happy* to make Mitchell's favorite meal for us, if only so his mother could go to her grave knowing that she's doing it properly, because there's a very good chance she isn't. Naturally, I'll help. I can be her sous chef—you know, to chop, chop, chop. And to direct and supervise her along the way. Then, all of us can enjoy a wonderful meal!"

She turned to me when she said that and leveled me with a glare. "You *do* know what Tank's favorite meal is, don't you?"

"I'm not sure he's ever told me," I said. And I meant it— Tank never had.

"Seriously?" Ethel said. "Are you really telling me that you don't know?"

"I'm sorry, but I don't."

"But he literally craves that meal whenever he comes home! He expects me to cook it for him. It's his grandmother's chicken pot pie. It's the one I served to you when you were here last. And you've never made it for him?"

"I'm afraid I haven't."

"I can't believe it," she said. "More than a year since my son has had his favorite chicken pot pie. Do you cook at all?"

Let's see, Ethel—when Jennifer and I first moved to Manhattan, I mastered ramen noodles because that's all we could afford. But I'm here to tell you that they were delicious! Beyond that, I can do a mean Lean Cuisine, I'm a pro when it comes to ordering takeout, I'm terrific at dining out, and I can make one hell of a martini. Other than that, I'm beyond good when it comes to feeding my zombies. In fact, I think one of them might like to take a bite out of you right now.

"Tank generally does the cooking," I said.

"He *what*?"

"He does the cooking. He says that it relaxes him."

"Oh, my word," she said. "I had no idea this was going on."

"It's not like it's the end of the world, Ethel," Harold said. "Tank has always enjoyed cooking—you know that."

"A woman should cook for the man in her life, just as I've always cooked for you." She looked at me. "Do you even know *how* to cook?"

When your son and I are in bed, Ethel, let's just say I certainly know how to heat up the sheets.

"Not really, no."

"Your mother didn't teach you?"

"There was never much time. I mean, she cooked for us, but she never really taught me how."

"Because everyone was so busy at the motel, I suppose."

"Yes."

"Then *I'll* teach you," she said with resolve in her voice. "But perhaps Harold is right. Since you are looking weirdly fatigued right now, *I'll* cook tonight, and you and I will cook tomorrow night. You must learn how to make that dish."

"I'd be happy to learn how."

And even as I said those words, I knew at once I'd soon come to regret them.

"Ethel? Harold?" called a voice from behind us.

"That's Stan," Ethel said. "He probably has Lisa's bags."

"Bring them into the kitchen, Stan!" Harold called out. And then he looked at his wife. "How about this? You have Stan take the bags up to the bedroom you've prepared for Lisa while I take her down to the gazebo. She came here to get married, Ethel, and I have a feeling the last thing on her mind right now is learning how to cook. But I bet she'd like to see where she and Mitch are going to get married." He looked over at me. "Would you like to see where?"

"Oh, I'd love to see the gazebo," I said. "I've been dying to see it."

"Then let me take you," he said. "Just the two of us."

"But what about me?" Ethel asked.

"You're officially on bag duty."

"Well!" she said. "Then by all means, do mind the ticks while you're in that meadow, because it's filled with them."

9

"It's so beautiful here," I said to Harold as we stepped out of the house and into the late-afternoon sun. As we walked around the front of the house, I admired the banks of flowers that surrounded it, all set deeply and thriving in dark mulch. I looked up at the bright-blue sky and knew that unlike in Manhattan, if I came out here at night, I'd actually see a blanket of stars mapping out the universe for me. And then there was the air itself, which was so clean and fresh I was once again reminded of Maine.

"I'm glad you like it here, Lisa," Harold said.

"I do. I'm glad Tank thought of getting married here. You know, if it weren't so flat, the landscape would remind me of where I grew up."

"Not many hills here," he said.

"It's just so *green*. Living in the city, you pretty much have to go to Central Park to see anything remotely like this. Otherwise, with the exception of a few other parks in the city, it's mostly nothing but skyscrapers or row upon row of buildings—residential and commercial."

"Do you like the city?" he asked.

"Of course I do," I said. "It's where I met your son."

I looked over at the seven massive barns far off to my left and thought they looked pristine. There had to be several hundred cattle grazing in the fields alongside them, which evoked in me a memory of my grandparents' farm in Harmony, Maine. Their farm wasn't nearly as large as this, but I nevertheless loved spending time there, if only to be with my grandparents—and also with my favorite cow, Annabelle. With the exception of Jennifer, for a good part of my youth, I'd considered Annabelle one of my closest friends and the most patient of listeners. It seemed silly to me now, but when I was a kid, the secrets I used to share with her had been profound.

After about a ten-minute walk on closely cut grass, we came upon the meadow itself, which had a wide, perfectly manicured path that stretched down the center of it before hooking off to the right.

"Tank wasn't joking," I said. "He'd said the gazebo and the pond were far from the barns. I can't even see them."

"We've got a ways to go yet."

"How many acres are there here?"

"About nine hundred."

"Nine hundred?"

"Something like that."

"You must love it here."

"I do," he said. "The work is hard, but as my father always used to say to me, hard work is good for the soul. God knows that's been said its share of times, but he was right, even if he was a soulless son of a bitch."

Startled by what he'd said, I just turned to him.

"Sorry," he said. "Ethel hates it when I swear, so I try not to do much of it around her, if only so she won't pray over my own soul. But I have to warn you, Lisa, sometimes I do have a mouth on me. I hope I didn't offend you."

"Harold, I write about zombies who eat people," I said. "You didn't offend me, because I have a mouth of my own, which I also need to keep in check."

"Not around me, you don't. But as for Ethel, that would probably be a smart move."

"That's been made very clear to me."

"I'm sure it has," he said with a roll of his eyes.

We kept moving forward along the mowed path as bees, flying insects, butterflies, and birds swept around the meadows on either side of us.

"You know," he said, "I wanted to take you alone to the gazebo for a reason, and that reason is Ethel. She hasn't been easy on you, Lisa. I'm sorry about that."

"Don't be," I said. "As tiny as I am, Harold, I'm surprisingly tough. And sometimes a little scrappy."

"You should be treated with respect."

"Ethel and I have had our moments, and I expect as we get closer to the wedding, we'll have a few more as the pressure rises. But I understand why she's sometimes the way she is. I'm marrying her only child, and she wants the best for him."

"She wants someone who can cook him that goddamned chicken pot pie, that's for sure."

I giggled when he said that, and for the first time that day, I felt the stress lifting off me just by being with him.

"I'll do my best to master it," I said.

"Even if you do, it still won't be enough for her."

"I get it," I said. "And I'll also get through it."

"You know, as much as I love her—and I do love her, Lisa, because believe it or not, Ethel is a good person, especially when she comes to trust you and love you, as she does

Mitch and me—I know firsthand how difficult she can be. She thinks she's about to lose Mitch to you, and that's hard on her—and I know she's taking it out on you in all kinds of underhanded ways. I'm sorry about that, too. I'll try to right the course when I can, although I might not always be around to do so. If she goes too far, just come to me, and I'll do my best to make things right, OK?"

"But if I did that, I'd just be ratting her out," I said. "And that alone would instill in her a sense of distrust, which is the last thing I want when it comes to our relationship. I'm trying to make her see that I really am the one for Tank, Harold. I love your son more than I think she understands."

"She knows it," he said. "She just doesn't want to admit it. She was terrible to you the first time you came here. I saw how she was behaving, and I should have said something to her right then and there. But it was Christmas, and I didn't want to fight with her, so please accept my apologies now for what happened then."

"I appreciate that," I said. "Just know that I'm going to try my best to turn things around between us."

"How was she when she picked you up at the airport?"

"Everything went fine until she made me listen to a certain audiobook."

"What audiobook?"

"If I remember correctly, I think it was called *Former Satanist Becomes Catholic*."

"Jesus H. Christ," he said to me. "That woman can't stop herself."

"It's fine. Actually, if I'm being honest, it was kind of entertaining."

"I think she has issues with the books you write."

"She does. But when she actually reads my books, she'll see that they probably aren't what she's expecting them to

be. My books aren't just about the undead eating people—
although there's plenty of that in them. At their core, they're
about the undead struggling with the idea that God
somehow left them behind to become something they can't
understand themselves. They feel abandoned by God. The
struggle over the loss of him. What Ethel doesn't know is
that religion plays a major role in my books. I think she'll
respond to that."

"Don't get your hopes up," he said. Then he pointed
ahead of him. "Now, how about if you look at that?"

I'd been so focused on him and our conversation that I
hadn't realized the gazebo and the pond had come into
sight. And what a sight it was. The gazebo was large and
oval, painted bright white, and had a two-tiered gray roof,
on the top of which was a metal cap adorned with a wooden
finial. All around it in dark-brown beds of mulch were
freshly planted annuals for color, several low flowering
bushes, many different varieties of hostas, and a host of
other plants.

Just behind the gazebo was the pond, which glistened in
the sunlight as several dozen swans glided regally through
the water, their graceful necks held just high enough to give
the impression that they felt the addition of this new gazebo
had nothing on their beauty. As I took it all in, I wished
Tank could be with me now so that we could have experienced this moment together. Already I missed the hell out
of him.

"It's amazing," I said when we finally came upon it. "And
the landscaping! That wasn't in any of the photographs
you sent."

"That's because Ethel just finished it a couple of days
ago. She wanted to surprise you with it."

I turned to him when he said that. "Ethel did this?"

"With some help, yes. But she planned out all of it. She's been working on it for the past two weeks. She chose every flower, plant, and bush. She wanted to make it beautiful, and since Ethel rarely fails when she sets her mind to something, she did."

"I'll have to thank her," I said. "It's remarkable what she's done. Is it OK for me to go up the steps and look around?"

"Sure it is," he said. "Now, how about if I leave you to your thoughts for a bit? I think you could probably use some time alone. What do you say?"

"Thank you, Harold."

"My pleasure, Lisa. Come back to the house when you're ready." He started to turn around to leave when I caught a gleam in his eye. "And don't forget..." he began.

"What's that?"

"Mind the ticks."

When Harold faded from sight, I reached into my pants pocket, removed my SlimPhone, and called Tank, who answered on the second ring.

"What are you wearing?" I asked.

"A pair of shorts. I just finished working out."

"You're not wearing a shirt?"

"As a matter of fact, I'm not."

"I bet you're sheathed with sweat," I said.

"You should see me."

"I wish I could," I said as I turned around and looked out at the pond. "I know I only left this morning, but I already miss you, Tank."

"I miss you, too. I wish I could be there with you."

"Especially now," I said, "because I'm standing in the

center of the gazebo, and it's beautiful, Tank. Way better in person than in the photographs your parents sent. Thank you for thinking of this. It's magical here."

"I thought you'd like it."

"I love it."

"How has Mom been?" he asked. "I've been worried."

"You mother is your mother, and she is who she is."

"What does that mean?"

I filled him in on my day with her.

"I can't believe she made you listen to that audiobook," he said.

"As I told your father, I actually didn't mind, because that shit was hilarious. And by the way, I adore your father."

"Dad's great," Tank said. "He's a straight shooter. As for my mother? She shoots from the side."

"And so she does."

"How do you feel about her reading your books?"

"All I hope is that she can look past the sensational aspects to see what the books are really about. Time will tell, I guess, because I'm sure she's going to be eager to share her opinions with me. I'll handle them as they come."

"Don't take any of her shit, Lisa."

"I promise to take only what I can swallow, nothing more. She tested my nerves once today—she knew she'd pissed me off, and when she sensed it, she backed down."

"I'm glad to hear that."

"We're getting married in a week, and I'm going to try my best to change her perception of me. I want her rooting for us when we get married, not disappointed that it's happening. I want her to feel that I really am the one for you. I'll try to make that happen, but as you know, I'm also no doormat. I have my limits, and I'll only accept so much from her."

"If she ever goes too far, you've got my full support to put her in her place."

"I appreciate that, but let's hope it doesn't come to that."

"Agreed. So, what else is happening?" he asked.

"I think the only thing I haven't told you is that Ethel is going to teach me how to make your favorite meal tomorrow, because she made it abundantly clear she was appalled that I haven't been serving it to you since we moved in together."

"What is she talking about?" he said. "What's my favorite meal?"

"Oh, come on," I said. "You could have told me. With Jennifer's help, I could have figured out how to make it."

"No—seriously," he said. "I don't have a favorite meal."

"You don't?"

"I don't. I don't know what she's talking about."

"What she's talking about is your grandmother's chicken pot pie."

He laughed when I said that. "Actually, I think that's *her* favorite meal. Not that it's bad, because Mom does know how to cook. Somewhere along the line, she must have gotten the impression that it was my favorite meal, because that explains why every single time I go home, she makes it for me. And like the good son I am, I eat it. And now she wants you to make it so she can test your cooking skills," he said. "She's probably setting you up, Lisa. You need to be aware of that."

"Believe me, I see what's coming, and even though I can't cook to save my life, I'll still try my best in an effort to appease her, which is pretty much mission impossible. The good news is that we don't have much time for this kind of petty shit because there's a wedding to put on, and very soon

I'll be focusing on that despite her clear and present efforts to sideline me."

"About the wedding," he said. "Do me a favor and look around you for a minute. Have they cleared enough of the meadow to allow for the seats and the tents, or is Dad holding off for that later in the week?"

"No, it's all been cleared," I said, looking out at the immaculate lawn in front of the gazebo. "There's a large space for everyone to sit, and beyond that must be where the two air-conditioned tents will go so you and your groomsmen can get ready in one while my girls and I get ready in the other. I wish you could see it, especially the flower beds your mother planted around the gazebo. They are epic. Your father told me she took charge of the project herself because she wanted it to be perfect—which it is. So, I'm more than happy to give her props for that. She went way out of her way for us, Tank."

"Is there enough room in the gazebo for everyone?"

"More than enough. I'm standing in the middle of it now, which is where the priest will stand. Looking out at our guests, I can see you to his right and me to his left. And then beside me will be Jennifer as my matron of honor, and then Blackwell, Daniella, and Alexa as my bridesmaids. To your left will be Alex as your best man, and then your uncle Sam, Cutter, and your cousin Taylor. There's plenty of room."

"Perfect."

"I should probably go," I said. "I have to unpack, and Ethel is likely wondering what's taking me so long. We'll be having dinner soon."

"How about if you call me later?" he said. "You know— tonight. When you're getting into bed."

"Of course I'll call and say good night."

"That's not exactly what I had in mind."

"What did you have in mind?"

"Maybe I want a little bit more than that."

I narrowed my eyes when he said that. "What are you up to?" I asked.

"Just because we're apart doesn't mean we can't keep things interesting."

"Are you talking phone sex?"

"What if I am?"

"But what if your parents hear me? You know how I am when you get me going. I become a siren!"

"I think we should do it," he said. "Come on. We can talk about all the things I'd like to do...starting with my mouth pressed between your legs."

"Now you're starting to turn me on."

"And that's a problem because..."

"Because I can't walk back to that house with my head-lights on."

"Come on, Lisa. Let me get you off later."

"Oh, my God..."

"You know you want to do it."

"I do. In fact, after today, you don't know how much I do."

"Then call me," he said. "Just before you turn in. My parents' bedroom is on the first floor and at the opposite end of the house from the bedrooms on the second floor, where you'll be. Believe me, they won't hear you. The house is too big."

"Are you sure?"

"I'm positive," he said. "I know that house, and it's built like a fortress."

"I have to admit it sounds kind of kinky," I said. "Think of it—me getting pseudo laid in the house that God built. How about if we up the ante? How about if we FaceTime it!"

"Seeing you naked would be even better."

"OK, so we're doing this. I'll call you around ten or so."

"I'll be up and waiting," Tank said. "With my hands full."

"You're terrible."

"Wait until you see *how* terrible."

I told him that I loved him and then turned off my phone and put it back in my pants pocket—but not before glancing down and noticing that my nipples had stiffened to the point that they were pressing against my tank. Since it was a long walk back to the house, I knew they'd settle down before I got there, so I took a breath, tried to relax, and started back up the mowed path.

10

By the time I'd returned to the house, my nipples had gotten themselves in check, even though my mind was racing with illicit thoughts of the clandestine evening Tank and I would have later—once I was certain Ethel and Harold were in bed and dead asleep.

Tank and I had never had phone sex before, let alone video sex, simply because we'd rarely been apart. So I had to wonder what this little experiment of ours would even look like.

I mean, where would I hold the phone? Near my little meow-meow, as Epifania liked to call it? Straight up against my breasts so Tank could see what he was missing? Or maybe video sex was all about the facial expressions I would make as we got each other off. Maybe it was all about me arching my back, rolling my eyes back into their sockets, and pulling at my hair as I went through variations of my O face.

And then I considered the lighting, which was critical, because nothing said sexy like a harsh glare against pale white skin. The lighting needed to be warm, seductive, and inviting. I hadn't seen my room yet, but I doubted the lights were on dimmers. Still, I was creative. I could always toss a light piece of fabric over a lamp to give the room a romantic glow.

As for what I'd wear later? Let's just say I was grateful I'd brought several sexy negligees with me for when Tank arrived later in the week, because otherwise I'd be screwed.

When I entered the house and walked toward the kitchen, I saw Ethel seated on the padded bench next to the large bay window that overlooked the front of the house. In her hands was the trade-paperback version of the first book I'd published with Wenn—*You Only Die Twice*. From the looks of it, she was almost halfway through it, which just underscored that Ethel McCollister was a fucking speed reader. I'd only been gone for a couple of hours, for God's sake, and she was burning through my book.

"Well, well," she said as she looked up at me. "And here I was thinking that you'd run away."

Thinking or hoping?

I decided to sidestep the jab.

"Ethel, I have to thank you," I said.

"Whatever for?"

"For all the work you did around the gazebo. Harold told me that you personally chose every flower, bush, and plant yourself, and that you oversaw the completion of all of it. It's beyond beautiful. Thank you for taking the time to do that for us."

"It was my pleasure, Lisa. I wanted everything to look just right."

"It does," I said.

"And I'm relieved. Now, tell me...because I have to tell you that I *have* been wondering—do you really believe in abortion?"

And already we're at it!

"Excuse me?"

"Abortion," she repeated. "Ripping an unborn child from a mother's womb." She tapped her index finger against the spine of my book. "I just finished a particularly upsetting scene in which one of your characters decides to have an abortion, and it got me to thinking—I wonder if Lisa would ever have one. Or, for that matter, if she's ever *had* one —not that it's any of my business, of course, but I have to say that you've made me wonder whether that's the case, particularly since that scene was so rich in detail. It seemed culled from personal experience. I'm hoping that isn't the case."

"I've never had an abortion, Ethel. And as for the scene you're referring to, the character in question had recently been bitten and become infected. She was dying, and she knew that when she passed, she would eventually turn into a monster capable of anything. She chose to have the abortion because she didn't know if her unborn child also had become infected through her blood or what she would do to it if she gave birth to it and it was healthy."

"Are you suggesting that she would have eaten her own child?"

"She might have, and she knew it. She had the abortion out of a desperate act of love for a child she'd never come to know."

"But if it hadn't become infected, certainly one of the survivors she's with could have taken it from her," Ethel said. "Kept it safe—made sure that it was loved. So, why didn't she consider that route? There was, after all, a chance that the baby might have been fine. She could have chosen life, couldn't she?"

"I suppose she could have, but that's not the direction I decided to take the book."

"Because you believe in the sin of abortion."

It wasn't a question—instead, it was a loaded statement. She was outright challenging me, but how far should I take this? Was she really looking for an argument already? Or was she just goading me to see how I'd react? Either way, if she kept this up, it could turn into an argument, which I didn't want to have, especially on my first day here.

Don't take any of her shit, Lisa. Tank's words echoed in the mind.

I promise to take only what I can swallow, but nothing more.

Those proved to be fateful words, because this? This was something I couldn't swallow. So, despite the inevitable consequences, I decided to take her on.

"I believe that my character did the right thing for her."

"But that doesn't answer my question."

"Then let me be clear, Ethel. I believe in a woman's right to choose."

"I thought so," she said. "All of you liberals do. As you've likely guessed by now, I believe in the sanctity of life."

Even though I was, in fact, a liberal, I nevertheless wanted to know how she'd labeled me as one. "What makes you think I'm a liberal?" I asked.

"Oh, I don't know, Lisa. Perhaps because of the scene we just spoke about. Or maybe it's due to your liberal use of taking the Lord's name in vain in print, which for the life of me I can't understand, since there are other ways to express one's displeasure. Or perhaps it's just your characters in general—at least in this book. I mean, they are a crude, scrappy lot, aren't they? I've skimmed through two sex scenes so far, and I'm only halfway through the book. Goodness knows what's to come."

"It's a book, Ethel. Fiction. Entertainment for the masses."

"Just fiction?" she asked pointedly. "You know, I once read somewhere that writing is an extension of one's personality. How do you feel about that? Any truth to it?"

"Absolutely."

"So, you would abort a child?"

"That would depend on the situation. But how about if we frame this another way, Ethel?"

"And what way is that, Lisa?"

"For a moment, how about if you give some thought to those cozy mysteries you read. Generally, a murder is involved, isn't that right?"

"Generally."

"Then let me ask you this—when you read those books, do you automatically assume that the writer is a murderer? That the idea that they wrote about a murder is an extension of *their* personalities and who *they* are as people? Or do you just read the books for enjoyment without giving a single thought to who wrote them and who they might be as human beings?"

"I see what you're doing," she said, reaching for the red ribbon on the windowsill next to her and wedging it into my book before snapping it shut. "You're deflecting."

"No, I'm not. In fact, I believe you're the one who just deflected. You can't have it both ways, Ethel. You can't judge me on my morality when you refuse to judge your favorite writers as you judge me."

"The women I read don't write about such filth," she said. "But you do."

I held up my hands when she said that before this truly escalated.

"That's enough," I said. "You and I are done for today. I'm tired. I need to unpack. And before long, I'll be going to bed."

"But there's dinner," she said as she stood up. "It's simmering on the stove."

What's simmering is me, lady, and trust me on this—you don't want to see me blow.

"I'm no longer hungry."

"Don't be ridiculous. We were just having a discussion."

"That was no discussion, Ethel. That was nothing but pure, unbridled judgment—yours, when it comes to how you view me. It's true, and you know it. Now, if you could show me to my room, I'll get settled in, I'll unpack, I'll try to forget about today and what's been said to me throughout the day, and hopefully we can start fresh tomorrow."

"Harold is going to wonder why you aren't at dinner. He's going to sense there's an issue."

"That's not my problem—it's yours. Besides, I'm sure you are absolutely capable of finding an excellent excuse for my absence that has nothing to do with the real reason I won't be at dinner."

"So, now you're calling me a liar?"

"Call it what you will." I leaned toward her, and when I did, her eyes widened. "You think you know me, Ethel, but you don't. Not even close. My hope is that you won't continue to judge this particular book by her cover, because you are way off when it comes to me. But enough of this. Please show me to my room. I'm tired, I'm going to turn in early—and frankly, I'd rather be alone than sit at dinner with you while you judge my manners and how I eat."

"I would do no such thing."

"We both know better. So, show me to my bedroom. I'll see you in the morning."

11

LATER THAT EVENING, after I'd unpacked my suitcases in the large guest room Ethel had prepared for me, my stomach growled, and I knew I'd be going to bed hungry due to the ridiculous conversation she'd baited me into having with her.

For a while, I'd half-expected Harold to come and check on me, but he hadn't, which told me that Ethel had successfully made him believe I really was too tired to eat and that I'd decided to unpack and go to bed early.

Whatever...

I was arranging my toiletries in the en suite bathroom when I checked the time on my watch and thought of Tank. It was half past eight, the sun had set, and a purplish twilight glow filled the bedroom with lavender-colored light. I went over to the three windows opposite my bed, drew the blinds, shut the curtains—and wondered if I had it in me to go forward with what Tank and I had planned for tonight.

If you don't, then she's really won the day. Is that what you want?

I thought about that for a moment, and I knew that of course it wasn't what I wanted. This was my wedding week, and while Tank might not be with me now due to circumstances neither of us could have predicted or prevented, that didn't mean we still couldn't be together—regardless of the method.

I've got to shake this off, I thought, looking at myself in the bathroom mirror. *I can't let her get to me...or ruin what could be a fun night with the love of my life. I owe it to Tank to give my all to him. So, fuck Ethel McCollister and her assumptions about me. Let her have them.*

With resolve, I went to the antique armoire across the room, opened its set of double doors, and removed a sexy lace teddy that would leave little to the imagination when I wore it. It was bright red and Tank had never seen me in it before, and as I turned it this way and that, I thought it would be perfect for tonight.

I laid it over the back of a chair and then looked around the bedroom with new eyes. As I had suspected, the lighting was way too harsh, but after grabbing a dark-brown hand towel from the bathroom and placing it over the lamp next to my bed, the room transformed itself into something that was perfectly lit and kind of sexy. The exception was the flowery bedspread, which looked as if Ethel had made it herself. With a flick of my wrist, it was gone, leaving clean, white sheets in its wake.

This isn't looking so bad...

And then I thought of my phone, which I hadn't charged since leaving New York. I grabbed it off a side table, turned it on, and saw that the battery was nearly dead. Quickly, I removed the charger from my carryon, found a socket next to the side table, and plugged the adapter in. The good news is that the phone charged quickly, so I'd likely just averted a crisis.

Shoes, I thought. *I need a pair of hot-looking shoes...*

I returned to the armoire and looked at all the shoes I'd brought with me. There were nearly a dozen of them, all lined across the bottom of the armoire. Most of them were perfectly appropriate for any occasion, one pair was for my wedding day, another pair was for the wedding rehearsal and the rehearsal dinner, and then there were the three pairs that were just sexy enough for those few evenings I'd spend with Tank when he arrived here after attending Brian's funeral.

For tonight, I decided to go with the Gianvito Rossi folie metallic leather ankle-wrap sandals with the four-inch heels, which Tank also hadn't seen. Plucking them out of the armoire, I placed them next to the bed. Before I headed off to take a shower, I went over to my bedroom door and saw with a jolt that there was no lock on it.

How can that be? I thought in horror. *No locks? Seriously?*

But what could I do about that? Nothing. So I just focused on the moment.

Time passed, and I made sure everything was just right in the bedroom. I looked at my watch, saw that it was nine, and wondered what time Ethel and Harold went to sleep. Or if they were already in bed now. I thought of opening the door to check for movement or conversation downstairs, but I didn't dare to. If one of them heard me, they might call up to me—which I didn't want, especially considering what Tank and I were about to do. Since my bedroom light was on, at the very least I wanted them to think I was simply in bed and possibly reading before I went to sleep.

I can't do anything with Tank if they're awake, I thought.

Too risky. Not worth it. But Tank will know when they generally turn in. And he'll also know the best way for me to check.

AFTER I'D SHOWERED, blown out my hair, and done my makeup, I wiggled into my skin-tight teddy before putting on my shoes, which proved a rather significant challenge, because I wasn't sure how to properly crisscross the straps around my ankles and up my lower calf.

When I'd finally figured it out, I sat back on the bed, stretched my legs out toward the ceiling, and kicked my feet a few times in the air as if I didn't have a care in the world. Then I hooked the shoes at their heels as I pressed my hand against my sex and closed my eyes in anticipation for what was to come.

Which hopefully would be both of us.

It was twenty minutes before ten when I remembered that I'd brought a bottle of Grey Goose with me in my carryon, knowing in my gut that I'd never find a drink here since the McCollisters didn't imbibe.

But I did.

Needing a shot of liquid courage if only to relax and to really get into the mood, I hurried over to the armoire and removed the bottle from the bag. Despite the fact that I had no ice to chill the vodka, at least there was a glass next to the sink. I poured myself a good inch, tossed it back, looked at myself in the mirror, fussed over my hair, added another layer of lip gloss, and then returned to the bedroom and reached for my phone. The battery was now at 90 percent, certainly powerful enough for what Tank and I had in mind.

Or maybe not, depending on how far we go...

Before I called him, I sat down on the bed, turned on the phone, and looked at myself in the camera as I positioned myself.

Not bad, I thought as I hoisted up the girls and fluffed out my hair. *The lighting is actually good.* I turned onto my stomach, moved the camera around so it was aimed at my ass, and then I craned my neck around so I could see what it looked like on the phone. *Oh, God*, I thought. *I'm beyond pale, but at least my ass is in shape, so there's that. But what to do about my hoo-ha? Do I even dare look at it through this thing? Is Tank even going to want me to go there? What if he does, and I haven't seen how it photographs first? Oh, Christ, I have to look.*

But I couldn't. I just couldn't. And so, after simulating a number of shots that I thought Tank would appreciate, I tapped his name in my contacts list and then pressed the video icon. Before I knew it, I was looking at Tank, who was lying shirtless in our bed—and who might even be naked, for all I knew—because his lower half was concealed by a sheet.

"You look amazing," he said to me. "I've been waiting hours for this."

"I hope I won't disappoint."

"Not considering what you're wearing. I've never seen you in that before."

"You were meant to see it while we were here. But since you can't be here, you're seeing it now." I lifted my legs and trained the camera toward my shoes. "And then there are these," I said. "Do you like?"

"The camera is kind of shaking," he said. "If you mean your legs, you know how much I love them—in fact, I'd like to run my tongue along the insides of your thighs right now."

"No, no—I mean the shoes. Do you like the shoes?"

"Right now, they're kind of a silverfish blur."

Fuck! I thought. *I'm so nervous, my hands are trembling.*

"How's that?" I said when I took hold of the phone with both hands.

"Very sexy."

I turned the camera back to my face.

"Tank, before we do anything, I need to know for sure that your parents are asleep. Because I can't do any of this without being absolutely sure they *are* asleep."

"That's easy," he said. "I already know that they're in bed. They always turn in around nine-thirty."

"I still need to be sure."

"All you need to do is open your bedroom door and see if the lights are on downstairs. If they are, one of them is up. But if they aren't, both of them have gone to bed."

"If one of them is up, they'll hear me—and question what I'm up to."

"You're being paranoid. You know how big the house is —no one's going to hear you part the door."

Your mother is like a hawk. If she's up, she will.

But I checked nevertheless.

"Pitch black," I whispered as I quietly closed the door again.

"Then they're in bed."

"What do we do now?"

"We have cybersex."

"Have you ever done this before?"

"Hell, no."

"Where do we even begin?"

"Just as I always begin with you," he said. "With my lips pressed against yours."

"Just so I'm clear on what you expect," I said, "do you want me to kiss the screen when you say something like that? Is that what I'm supposed to do? Or am I supposed to do something else?"

"You're supposed to listen to me, Lisa. You're supposed to let yourself go, just as I'm about to, and we're going to look at each other while we talk to one another."

"Look at which parts of each other?"

"Right now, think of this first part as foreplay. Think of us as being in the same room together with you in my arms. You know, with you melting into me, like you usually do."

"I can do that," I said.

"Close your eyes."

I closed them.

"Imagine my mouth against yours."

I did—and I felt my body tingle with a rush of sense memory. Nobody in my life had ever kissed me the way Tank kissed me. Whenever our lips touched, I could always feel his love for me, which was transcendent. And that's what I felt now as I imagined his lips on mine.

"You're off camera," he said.

In my delirium, my left hand had moved slightly to the left. I righted it and pointed the phone at my face. "Sorry."

"You look beautiful tonight," he said.

I looked up at him in my SlimPhone and thought he looked hot. And then I thought that this was kind of like porn! He was leaning on his side in our bed, but unlike me, there was no phone in his hands. In fact, his right hand was busy smoothing over one of his massive pecs as he grinned disarmingly into the camera. From where he was lying, I could clearly see that he'd somehow propped his phone on my nightstand and had pointed it horizontally at him so that I could see the length of him. Why hadn't I thought of that?

Does it matter? Just go with it. Have fun!

"Why are you partly covered with a sheet?" I asked.

"Why do you ask?"

"Because it's cruel of you."

"How is it cruel?"

"I think you know why."

"Tell me why."

"Because I love seeing you naked," I said.

"Do you want to see more of me?"

"I always want to see more of you."

"I could say the same thing to you. But let's take this slowly. Why don't you take your free hand and suck on your index finger for me?"

Excuse me...what was that? Since when do I suck on my index finger? By talking to each other like this, are we about to reveal more about our fantasies than we ever would have if we were making love in person, which generally is without much conversation—if any at all?

I didn't know, but when it came to having sex with Tank, I was open to pretty much anything, because I loved him and trusted him. So, I slid my index finger into my mouth and started to gently suck on it.

"Mmm," I said.

"What does it taste like?"

Vodka.

"You," I said.

"Now, take that finger, dip it beneath your negligee, and rub it over one of your nipples."

When I did, I felt a sense of excitement and surprise overcoming my body as it responded to the touch of my moistened finger. Tank had me put my finger in my mouth for a reason. With it so wet, it felt more erotic.

"Now, pinch it," he said. "Hard."

When I did, it felt as if he himself was doing it.

"I want you to imagine my mouth between your legs," he said. "You know how that feels. You also know how deep I can go."

I knew exactly how deep he could go.

"Think of me down there right now."

"I want to touch myself," I said in frustration. "But I can't when I'm holding this phone over my head."

"Then take the pillow next you, place it beside you, and position the phone so I can see all of you—and so that you can see all of me."

I followed his suggestion, and with my hands finally free, I felt liberated to take this to the next level. I turned my head to look at him just as I reached down to touch myself. Meanwhile, Tank removed the sheet to reveal his erection to me, which inflamed me because I wanted him inside of me. For several moments, each of us just looked at the other as we pleasured ourselves before I rolled onto my side so he could see my ass.

"I wish you could slap it," I said.

"So do I. Why don't you do it for me?"

I did. And then I smacked it again.

"This is hotter than I thought it would be," Tank said.

"Speaking of hot," I said. "*I'm* getting hot." I sat up and pulled down the top of my teddy so he could see my breasts, which were so full with arousal that my nipples looked as if they wanted to reach through my phone's screen and present themselves directly into Tank's mouth.

"Christ, you're beautiful," he said as he grabbed a fistful of his cock.

"I want your cock," I said. "I want it in my mouth."

"It's in your mouth."

"But it's too big for my mouth."

"You've taken it before. Take it again."

"I'm taking it now," I said as I lifted my legs high into the air. I slipped my right hand down the front of my teddy and began to lightly brush my fingers over my clit before I pressed two fingers inside of me—and began to lose control.

"Think of me inside you," he said in a low growl. "Gently at first, but then rougher as you open yourself up to me."

"That's right," I said as I closed my eyes. "You're on top of me. You're kissing me. Now your mouth is on one of my breasts. The right one," I said as I cupped my free hand over it. "Your breath is hot against me. You're biting my nipple."

"How about if you bite mine?"

"I'm biting it."

As our conversation escalated with a feverish pace, I could feel myself growing wet with lust as I started to soar toward climax.

"Fuck me," I said. "Come on, Tank—fuck me."

"I'm fucking you."

"Fuck me harder!"

"I'm fucking you harder."

"Really plow into me."

"I'm seriously plowing into you."

"And I'm grabbing your ass. I'm pulling you closer to me. Fuck me, Tank! Get me there. I'm close."

"Grab the base of my cock and pull every inch of me into you."

"I just did!" I said in a raised, heated voice. "And it feels amazing."

"You're so fucking wet," he said.

"I am! And you're so big! And I feel so tight! And this is

happening in Ethel McCollister's house! I'm taking her son's big cock while she's having nightmares of abortions and evil and all the things that I'm not! I'm getting close!"

"Lisa..." he said. "What the hell?"

As I inserted another finger into me, pinched one of my nipples and turned into a heated silo of sex unleashed, I writhed upon the bed before I looked over at Tank. "Come with me," I said. "Come on, Tank—shoot that big load of yours all over me. Or inside of me. Wherever you want to put it, I'll take it. But you need to do it soon, because I'm really fucking close."

"What was that about—?"

"Do you want to see how close? Yes? Then let me show you how close," I said as I stood up and removed my teddy before I lay back down on the bed. I lifted up my legs, parted them as wide as I could, and then grabbed the phone and pointed the camera straight at my sex as I inserted my fingers into me.

"Holy shit," he said. "You've lost control."

"I needed to," I said. "Especially after today. Now fuck me! Please! Just fuck the living shit out of me! Because right now, I'm getting fucked in the house that Ethel's God built— and by her own son! And it's never felt so good!"

When I said that, a brisk rap came at my door. In shock and in horror, I swung my head around just as Ethel entered the room with a tray of food in her hands. When she saw me naked with my phone about a foot away from my privates, her eyes widened, she swayed to the left, and her shoulder struck the doorjamb. Then her lips curled back in a kind of distorted horror.

"What on earth are you doing?" she exclaimed.

"What's going on?" I heard Tank say. "Is that my mother?"

"It *is* your mother," Ethel said as she glared at me. "And both of you are defiling my house! You've turned it into a den of iniquity!"

"What are you doing here?" I asked as I sat up, tossed the phone to my side, and quickly gathered a sheet around myself. "That door was closed for a reason."

"So I can see!"

"You can't just walk in here, Ethel. You can't just—"

"*I can do whatever I want in my own home!*"

"Then maybe it's best if I stay at a motel!"

"If this is how you're going to behave, maybe it's best that you do!"

"Mom, you need to listen to me," Tank said from the SlimPhone. "Lisa and I are adults. We're in a committed relationship. And you need to leave right now, because none of this is your business."

"*None of this is my business?*" she asked in a weirdly piercing shrill. "*None of this is my business?* Are you serious, Mitchell? Do you even know what I just walked into? A bordello, that's what! A palace of porn!"

As rage took hold of her body—and her eyes darkened against me—the tray she was holding started to shake in her hands.

"And to think I was lying in bed feeling *guilty* about the conversation we had earlier," she said to me. "To think that I couldn't sleep because of it! I know you haven't eaten anything since you left Manhattan, which was bothering me since you chose not to eat dinner with us after our little chat about the contents of your book. So I decided to get up and make you a perfectly nice chicken-salad sandwich, Lisa. I even poured you a glass of milk. I was concerned about you, and what do I get for that concern? You filming yourself in ways that are so lewd and unspeakable that I want to vomit."

"Leave the room, Mom," Tank said with a sudden sternness in his voice. "Do it now, because I've heard enough. And so has Lisa."

"*Fine*," she said as she walked over to my bureau and slammed the tray down on top of it. "There's your sandwich, Lisa. And your milk. Consider them power fuel for the rest of your nightly adventures with my son, because you probably need them right now just to get through God only knows what's coming next. But as for this? As for what I just walked into? The fact that I just witnessed my own son naked and heated and being drawn into your strange sexual fantasies? This I can't have. This I *won't* have. So, here's where we stand now, girl. As you saw on the drive from the airport, there are plenty of motels and hotels between Prairie Home and Lincoln. I'll have a list of them waiting for you in the morning, and somebody will drive you to one of them, since I clearly can't have you here when you and my son will only be doing *this*." She stalked toward the door, walked through it, and said a blistering "*Good night*" before slamming the door behind her.

"LISA," I heard Tank say from the SlimPhone. "Pick up the phone. Look at me. It's going to be all right. I'll make sure of it. I'll call her in the morning and work this out."

With the sheet held close to my naked breasts, I was in such a state of shock that I just stared straight ahead at the tray of food Ethel had left on the bureau, and I felt nauseous just looking at it.

I'm finished, I thought. *That's the end of me when it comes to her. I'm done—and it took me less than a day to pull it off, so congratulations to me. She'll never accept me after what she just saw. That image of me lying flat on the bed with my legs spread wide and the camera down there to capture it all for Tank will be burned into her mind for the rest of her life —particularly whenever she lays her eyes on me. And what is she going to tell Harold, my only ally here? How is this going to change my relationship with him? Because it will. I know it will. Even he won't be able to look past this. What have I done?*

"Lisa, come on. Pick up the phone. Talk to me, for God's sake."

I picked up the phone and looked at him. He was sitting on the edge of the bed with a sheet wrapped around his waist. I caught a glimpse of the scar on his chest left by the bullet he'd once taken for me, and I knew he was about to take another bullet for me, especially if he planned to talk to Ethel in the morning.

"Your mother didn't like me before, Tank, and after walking into that? There's no saving our relationship now. She's never going to forgive me for this."

"I can talk to her," he said.

"And say what? That she should unsee what she saw? That's not going to happen. And since I know it's not going to happen, I'm leaving in the morning. I'll go to a motel. I can't be expected to stay in a house where I'm not wanted. Or where I'm always going to be judged as your horrible choice for a wife. That's where I stand, and I need your support when it comes to my decision."

"You're going to get my support in ways you've never imagined," he said. "But before you do anything, at least let me talk with her first, because this isn't just on you. I'm also complicit in this. If she's going to judge you, then she's also going to have to judge her own son, because I was a happy and willing partner tonight. Christ, I was having some harmless fun with my future wife, and I won't apologize for it."

"You'll never get through to her, Tank. You won't."

"That's not necessarily true."

"I think it is, and here's why—you didn't see how she looked at me. You didn't see the disgust on her face or the hatred in her eyes before she left. Her loathing of me was palpable. And here's the thing," I said, "I don't blame her, especially after walking in on that. If I were in her shoes, I can only imagine how I'd be feeling right now."

"I'm sorry," he said. "For all of it. I was the one who came up with the idea of doing this, and trust me, she'll hear that from me. I'll put it all on me. We did nothing wrong."

"I disagree," I said. "We thought we could get away with this in her house, which we didn't. She's religious. She's made no bones about it. We should have respected that. What in the hell were we thinking?"

"Had I been with you now, we would have made love in that bedroom. My mother and my father would have known that, and they would have said nothing about it. So who gives a damn if we tried to do it by phone?"

"Your mother asked me whether I've ever had an abortion today, Tank."

"She did *what*?"

"You heard me. She's reading the first book I published through Wenn. And because of that, when I returned from the gazebo after talking with you, she took me on. She asked me all of these invasive questions, such as whether I've ever had an abortion or if I even believed in abortion. She hammered me with judgment—and also with a sense of self-righteousness that put me on the defensive."

"What did she say to you?"

I told him—and I also told him what I'd said to her.

"She deserved every word of it," he said.

"But here's the thing, Tank—not only did she do it on purpose, but she did it on my first day here. She didn't even give me a day or two to settle in before she started her attacks on me. She went straight for my jugular on the drive from the airport with that ridiculous audiobook she made me listen to. And later today, when she was in the middle of reading *You Only Die Twice*, she went straight for the abortion issue, which turned the moment so caustic between us that I skipped dinner. She has an agenda when it comes to me, and I think that agenda is now abundantly clear. She doesn't want this wedding to happen. I think that in some twisted, fucked-up way, she's trying to shove me out of your life while she still can without you here to stop her."

"That's not going to happen."

"I know it's not going to happen. But try telling her that."

"I plan to."

"She might pretend to listen to you and to understand all that you have to say to her, but that's going to be all talk. Things won't change until you get here. She's only going to make this week worse for me, which I won't have. I'm out of here tomorrow."

"Maybe I should just forget Brian's funeral and get to Prairie Home now."

"No," I said firmly. "You will go to your friend's funeral. That's already been settled, and I won't have it any other way. His wife and children need you to be there for them. And then there's you—you also need to be there to pay your respects to your friend. I know how important that is to you, so not going is off the table as far as I'm concerned."

"Lisa, I know you want this wedding to be perfect."

"I do."

"But if you leave my parents' house, who is going to be

there to make certain that you get the wedding you want? That all the details are attended to? Because if you do leave, it's going to be my mother making those decisions, which I know you don't want."

"I'll call Jennifer and Blackwell," I said. "I'll tell them everything that's transpired since I got here. They are my best friends, and they'll drop everything to step in to take care of this for us. When I find a motel, I'll call them from my room, and I can guarantee you they will be on a plane as soon as possible. Because I know in my heart that I mean as much to them as they mean to me. They will have my back when it comes to this. They will intervene, and Blackwell alone will handle your mother far better than I can. I mean, come on—imagine Ethel up against her."

"It's not going to come to that," he said. "Please let me talk to her before you make a decision. I know how to get her in line."

"How?"

"I'll make things very clear to her. She either treats you with respect, or I'll tell her that we'll ditch our plans to get married at home. Since our friends and family already have plans to travel to Prairie Home, we'll need to get married at one of the churches in town so we don't inconvenience them, which won't be an issue. But she won't be invited to the wedding, and I'll tell her so. I'm her only son—her only child, for Christ's sake—and that should be enough to wake her the fuck up when it comes to us."

"Tank, I don't want to be the person who drives a wedge between you and your mother. I know that you are close to her. I don't want to bear that burden. I think it's better that I just leave in the morning and bring in Jennifer and Blackwell."

"How about this?" he said. "After I talk with her and if I

feel that I've failed to turn this around, I'll text you either way. And then you'll know exactly what to do."

That sounded reasonable enough, so I capitulated.

"All right," I said. "Give it a go, I guess. But if your mother doesn't do a complete one-eighty by morning when it comes to how she treats me, I will be out of here, Tank. If things don't go well between you two, I'll book a nearby church, and I'll call in my friends to help me with the details. She needs to understand that our wedding isn't dependent on having it at her home."

"Lisa, I'm sorry about this."

"Don't be," I sighed. "We both knew what we were getting into when I came here alone. What neither of us understood is where we'd end up in just one day. We're in this together, Tank. And however this goes down, we will get married on Saturday."

"Do me a favor?"

"I'd do anything for you."

"My mother gets up around five. Don't leave your room until you've received a text from me. Since we both know she'll be eavesdropping after I contact her, we'll communicate via text, and I'll give you my best opinion on what you should do when you walk down those stairs. I won't bullshit you, Lisa—I never have, and I never will. If I think it's best that you leave and call in the reinforcements, I'll tell you to do so. But if I think I've gotten through to my mother and that you should stay, I'll also tell you that."

"You've got one hell of a fight ahead of you, Tank, especially if you think she's going to change enough for me to want to stay here."

"Let me have that fight," he said.

"If you want."

"I'll get her to back down, Lisa. I have my ways."

And I needed to trust him on that, so I just shrugged at him. "I love you, Tank."

"I love you, Lisa. And I'm sorry about tonight."

"Don't be," I said. "All I want is for each of us to get a good night's sleep, and then we'll see what tomorrow brings. I'll be up and waiting for your text. And I'll do as you suggest. And then?" I just cocked my head at him. "I guess we'll take it from there."

12
———

AFTER A RESTLESS NIGHT of tossing and turning, I awoke the next morning at four-thirty feeling weirdly awake. Despite yesterday's series of exhausting events, I should have felt too tired to even get out of bed—but I didn't.

Instead, I was wired. My circuits were already on high alert.

I turned on my side, reached for my cell on the bedside table, and checked to see if Tank had texted me. He hadn't, likely because he wanted to leave me alone until he had a definitive decision on how I should go forward today.

I longed for a cup of coffee, but I knew I couldn't have one without going downstairs—which wasn't about to happen. So, I decided to take a long, hot shower instead, one that lasted a good fifteen minutes as I let the water beat against my tense shoulders, back, and neck. When I was finished, I toweled off and slipped into my white robe, leaning against the vanity as I looked at myself in the mirror.

I thought I looked like shit.

There were bags beneath my eyes—but none of them

were designer, that's for sure. As light-skinned as I was, I thought I looked unusually pale this morning, even though I should have been pink from the heat of the shower alone. When I'd left Manhattan yesterday, I hadn't looked anything like this. But now? After spending not even twenty-four hours with Ethel McCollister, I looked like one of my undead characters.

While I waited for Tank to text me, I went through the motions of pulling myself together with a whole host of potions that would help me look my best before I faced Ethel and Harold. And I did it all, leaning hard on all I'd learned from Bernie—full makeup, flat-ironed hair, and bold red lips that clearly stated that if you fucked with me today, I would rip out your heart and happily eat it.

With some fava beans.

Since I didn't want it to look like I was trying too hard, I chose a pair of casual white capris and a navy tank to complete the look. On my feet I wore a pair of flats—in case I needed to get out of here fast.

And when I was done? I poured the milk Ethel had offered to me the night before into the sink, and returned the glass to its tray on the bureau next to the sorry-looking sandwich. Then I just watched the time pass by as I paced with my phone in my hand, knowing that since it was now ten past five, Tank was likely talking to his mother now.

What is he saying to her? I thought. *How is she taking it?*

At five-twenty, my cell phone dinged, alerting me to a text. I immediately switched on my phone and read what Tank had sent.

"After that talk, I think you'll be fine today, tomorrow, and straight through to our wedding," he wrote. "I was very clear with her—she's not to judge you, she's to be polite to you, and she's not to fuck with you. I took a hard line with her, Lisa, and given the tone of my voice, I know she heard me. She knows that if she has just one more misstep with you, you will indeed go to a motel, we will have our wedding elsewhere in Prairie Home, and she won't be invited. Text me back if you need to. I'm here for you. I love you—Tank."

So, he went there, I thought as I typed out a text. *Maybe this will finally end this ridiculousness between Ethel and me...*

"Did she tell Harold what she saw?"

"She did. I also spoke with him. As usual, my father is unfazed."

But is he really unfazed? I wondered. *Or is he just putting on a good front for you, Tank, because he loves you?*

I knew I'd likely never know the answer to that question, and that upset me, because I genuinely liked Harold—and I wanted him to like me.

"All right," I texted. "I'll see what happens, and we'll take it from there."

"If she steps out of line again, you walk."

"I will," I wrote. "I love you, Tank. Wish me well. I'll admit that I'm nervous about facing her right now."

"I understand that, but just be you, Lisa—the woman I fell in love with. If that isn't enough for her, then the repercussions are on her. Text me as soon as you can, and let me know how things are going."

"I will—talk later. XOXO."

It took half an hour before I got up the nerve to pick up the tray and take it downstairs into the kitchen, where God only knew what faced me.

"WELL, GOOD MORNING," Ethel said as I stepped into the kitchen. She was standing at the sink, and I saw in a quick glance that she was wearing her own armor—a full face of makeup, hair washed and blown out, a pretty white shirt that complimented her tanned complexion, and slim-fitting khakis.

"Good morning, Ethel," I said.

"I had a feeling you also were an early riser," she said as she started toward me. "Here on the farm, we have to be, as I imagine you had to be when you worked all those years at your parents' motel. Harold's already had his breakfast and is working in the barns with the rest of the boys. This morning, it's just us."

Was that a threat? I wasn't sure. Her voice sounded pleasant enough, but since I didn't trust her, I honestly didn't know what I was walking into.

Give this a chance, I thought. *You said you would.*

"Here, let me take that for you," she said as she took the tray from my hands. "And let me cook something for you. You must be famished—and don't tell me that you're not."

I was beyond hungry, so I just nodded at her when she turned to me with expectant eyes.

"What would you like to eat?"

"Toast?" I said. "Maybe a cup of coffee?"

"You have to be hungrier than that. Do you like eggs? Because I make the *best* eggs."

"Have you eaten yet?"

"Yes, with Harold. But it's no problem, Lisa. Let me make breakfast for you, and then you and I can start talking about the wedding. Because we have a lot to do before the big day. When Tank arrives later in the week, you and he will meet Father Harvey together, so we don't need to worry about that right now. But you and I have one major to-do list to get through, which includes deciding where the tents will be constructed, going to the florist to make sure the flowers you've chosen are just right, going to the caterer to make certain we've missed nothing when it comes to the rehearsal dinner...and then there's the cake, which is so critical that I think you should meet the woman who is making it for you. And since there are so many other things to do, you need your energy. So, how about coffee, toast, and a couple of eggs made any way you like?"

Who are you? I thought, looking at her in wonder.

"That would be lovely," I said.

"Then let me get the coffee started. How would you like your eggs? Poached? Fried? Scrambled? Baked?"

"Scrambled," I said.

"Done. Now, have a seat at the kitchen table, and let me get to work. Everything will be finished in a matter of minutes."

And it was. As she sat opposite me with a cup of coffee of her own, I had to admit the eggs were delicious.

"Thank you," I said when I was finished. "That was amazing."

"Later today, you and I will cook Tank's favorite dish—his grandmother's famous chicken pot pie. I can't wait to show you how to make it."

"I'm terrible when it comes to making pastry," I said.

"Don't worry about it. Many people think making pastry is difficult, but it really isn't. I have a foolproof way of making it. You'll see. I use my food processor, and it comes out perfect every time. The secret is using cold cubes of butter and then letting the pastry rest for thirty minutes in the refrigerator before rolling it out. Other than that, the rest of the dish is just as easy. I'll walk you through all of it, and the three of us will have it for dinner tonight."

"Ethel," I said. "We should probably discuss last—"

"Let's not," she interrupted. "I don't think that would be

good for either of us. Let's consider this a new day and also a new page. Shall we turn that page together, Lisa? Because our book is going to have a great ending. It's going to have the *best* ending. Tank told me so this morning."

Why don't I believe that?

She smiled sweetly at me, but her smile wasn't reflected in her eyes. Instead, her eyes seemed weirdly intense to me, as if behaving kindly to me was somehow poisoning her.

"You'll see," she said. "Everything's going to be fine. I promise!"

"Before we start in, would you mind if I take a walk around the grounds? I'd like to stretch my legs and take advantage of the sun and the fresh air."

"Of course not," Ethel said. "Go and have a walk. Visit the gazebo. Say hello to the swans for me. Get yourself some fresh air and some exercise, and then we'll dig in."

"Thank you for breakfast," I said as I stood from the table. "It really was wonderful, Ethel."

"My pleasure. How long do you think you'll be gone?"

"Maybe an hour?"

"Perfect—just enough time for me to clean up and do some laundry. I'll see you when you return."

When I left the house, I had one mission in mind— finding Harold and seeing where I stood with him.

When I finally spotted him, he was in the third barn from the house and surrounded by three men. I heard a low moaning that sounded to me like an animal in pain. Since this barn was filled with cows, it occurred to me that one of them was under some sort of duress.

"Take it easy, girl," I heard Harold say as I walked toward

him and the other three men. They were standing in a pen looking down at something I couldn't see. "Everything's going to be all right."

"Harold?" I said as I neared them.

He looked up at me when I said his name, and then he quickly waved me over. "Mable's about to give birth. Come quick. You need to see this, Lisa, because it's something you'll never forget."

When I reached the pen and saw the large brown cow lying on its side with one of its back legs extended as she pushed, he motioned to the men around him. "Scotty, Mark, and Luke—this is Lisa, my son's fiancée."

"Pleasure to meet you," I said to them as I shook their hands. I looked at Mable, who seemed distraught, and then turned back to Harold. "Is she going to be OK?"

"It's her first—we'll see. But she's a strong girl, so I'm betting on her."

"Betting on her? Could something go wrong?"

"Anything can go wrong, but it generally goes right."

Generally?

"Can I do anything?" I asked.

"Just offer her your support. Talk to her if you want. Soothe her with that pretty voice of yours, which is a whole lot more gentle than ours. I think she'd rather like that."

Since I loved animals, that was easy for me.

"Mable," I said as I watched her head lift and fall on her bed of hay. She was an enormous cow—probably a Jersey from what I could tell—but as strong as she likely was, she was perhaps now at her most vulnerable and exposed. She was panting, moaning, and struggling, which made my heart ache for her, because this moment of giving life was a life she herself hadn't known existed until now. "We're with you, sweetie. We are—and all of us are rooting for you right now. This can't be easy for you, but you do have to push, and then we'll all take a big breath before you push again."

Mable clocked me with a sidelong glance when I said that. I felt the pain in her gaze, and then she looked away and started to cry out again. But when she did, she also pushed, and three things appeared at once—two hooves and the beginnings of one flaring snout.

"Well, shit," Harold said as he looked at me. "You might be a damned cow whisperer, Lisa, and you don't even know it. Because from what the boys have told me, she went into labor last night. I've been with her for the past hour, and none of us have gotten her this far. Keep talking to her. She's responding to your voice. Let her hear it and be supported by it."

"Can I touch her?" I asked.

"Best not to. Just talk to her."

"Mable," I said to her in a low, coaxing voice as I hunched down on my knees. "You're about to give birth to your first calf. Come on, girl. Give us another push. You can do it. I know you can."

When Mable twisted her body on the hay and pushed again, her calf suddenly slid halfway out of her as she reared her backside up into the air. For a moment, Harold just looked at me in surprise. "I should hire you," he said, "because you're making brisk work of this. Mable is clearly responding to you."

"I don't know about that," I said. "If she's been in labor since last night, I just happened to come along at the right moment. I think we should give Mable the credit here, not me."

"Bullshit," one of the men said. "She's listening to you."

I turned around and saw that it was Luke who had said that. He was a good-looking young man in his earlier twenties with sandy-brown hair and hazel-green eyes. He was wearing jeans, a dirty white T-shirt, well-worn leather boots, and a cowboy hat.

"Shouldn't be long now," he said. "It'll go quick at this point. Talk to her again, Lisa."

I did, and as I did, the last few moments did go fast as Mable kept lifting her bottom until the calf slipped out.

"It's a bull," Harold said. "And a big one. No wonder she was having such a hard time. Step back before she stands up, Lisa. Let's give her some room now."

"Is the calf OK?" I asked. "It's not moving."

"Looks fine to me," he said as Mable struggled to stand before she started to wash her newborn with her tongue. As she did, I saw that Harold was right—the calf started to respond to its mother's touch. Its eyes opened and blinked, it lifted its head with an effort, and then it let out a small grunt as Mable continued to clean it.

With the exception of Jennifer's birth, it was one of the most beautiful things I'd ever witnessed.

"Lisa, would you like to name him?" Harold asked.

"Are you sure it's a boy?"

"No two ways about it."

"Then how about Nico?" I said.

"Nico?" he said. "Why Nico?"

"Because one day, he's going to be popular with all the girls on the farm—and being named Nico won't hurt one bit. Trust me."

"So, Nico it is. Luke, you watch over Mable and Nico for a couple of hours. Scotty and Mark, back to it."

"Yes, sir," they said in unison.

"Now," Harold said to me, "I have a feeling you didn't come looking for me to see a cow give birth, although I hope it was a new experience for you."

"It was amazing," I said as I watched Mable tend to her new calf. "My grandparents had a farm, but I never saw any of their livestock give birth. I can't believe I just witnessed that."

"Nature does its thing, and so did Mable—with your cow-whispering help, of course."

He held out his hand to me, I walked over to him and took it in my own, and we walked outside, where hundreds of cows were grazing in the sprawling fields that stretched out before us. Well beyond them, I saw what appeared to be thousands of chickens free-roaming the land.

"So, what's on your mind, kiddo?" he asked. "Let me guess—last night? Because if this is about last night, you and I have nothing to talk about, other than I'm glad my son is with a woman who's willing to take on his creative cellphone suggestions in an effort to make both of you happy."

Tank really had told them everything. I didn't know whether to cringe or be grateful. Like Mable just moments ago, I also felt vulnerable and exposed.

"Ethel made a big deal of it because that's who she is, but I need you to know that I'm not her, Lisa. Whatever she walked into last night doesn't concern me, it shouldn't concern her, and I don't want it to ever concern you. Because frankly, there's nothing to be concerned about. I know you're the right woman for my boy—I've seen it in how you two look at each other. I also know that at some point, when my wife finally gets over the stupid idea that she's going to lose her son to another woman, she'll see what I see in Mitch and you: a great match."

"Is that what this is about?" I asked him. "She thinks that because Tank and I are about to get married, he won't continue to be there for her?"

"I think so. I think Ethel loves Mitch more than she loves

me. Not that she doesn't love me, because I know she does. But ever since the day he was born and the doctor told her she couldn't have another child, Mitch has always been her world."

"Her doctor told her she couldn't have another child?"

"He did, and for personal reasons that even Mitch doesn't know about." He looked at me for a long moment and then appeared to come to a decision. "Ethel miscarried twice before she had Mitch. When she found out that she was pregnant with him, she started to pray every day that this would be the one. We both wanted a child more than anything, and I think the pressure she felt to give us one was one of the reasons she started to go to church. For a while, she practically lived there—at least until the pregnancy got so bad that she was ordered to take bed rest for the last several months of her term."

"I'm so sorry," I said. "I had no idea about any of this."

"Ethel believes that without prayer, she would have lost Mitch just like she'd lost the others. And you know what? Who am I to judge, because she might be right. That woman prayed every day, and in the end, we got our son."

"Tank knows nothing about this?" I said.

"He doesn't. And that's Ethel's choice. She sees those miscarriages as failures—deep signs of her own weakness, likely something that could have been prevented if she'd just turned to the church earlier. After we had Mitch, we never discussed them again, because it was too painful for her to think about all that we had lost. Instead, we were just grateful for what we had, and that was Mitch."

And there it was—the reason Ethel was so protective of Tank—and also why she was so religious. But did any of that give her the right to judge me? To taunt me? To make things so difficult for me? No. It was terrible what Ethel had gone through, but I shouldn't be the one bearing the brunt of it.

"Now, listen to me," he said. "I'm only telling you this so you can have a better understanding of her. She's fiercely protective of Mitch, and now you know why. Whatever's going on between you two has nothing to do with you, Lisa. Because believe me, if Mitch was with another girl, she'd be going through the same bullshit you're going through. With that said, is it an excuse for any of her behavior toward you? No, it isn't. After she and I got off the phone with Mitch this morning, I told her myself that she needed to lay off you or we'd lose Mitch. Because after that phone call from Mitch this morning, I'm here to tell you that he let his mother have it. If she's smart, she won't want to cross him after that. But when it comes to Ethel, I also know that I can't promise you she won't. She might go after you again. You need to be prepared for that."

"I was going to leave today," I said to him. "I was planning to go to a motel."

"I wouldn't have blamed you if you had. I would have driven you to one myself, even though I would have missed having you here. My hope is that you will stay. My other hope is that Ethel will give you the respect you deserve."

"But what if she doesn't?"

He shrugged at me, and I saw in his wary blue eyes that even he wasn't sure how Ethel would behave going forward.

"If she doesn't, you're either going to have to go to a motel and have your wedding elsewhere, or you'll have to have it out with her," he said. "She knows what's on the line here—being denied going to her own son's wedding. If she's foolish enough to risk that by continuing to provoke you, then that's on her, and she'll get what she deserves. What Ethel went through thirty-some years ago doesn't excuse her behavior now, Lisa. I just told you about her past so you could have a better idea of who you're dealing with and how she became the woman she is today."

"I'll never say a word about any of it," I promised. "Not to Tank. Not to anyone. But thank you for telling me, Harold, because at least it gives me some insight. I'm very sorry for your own losses."

"In the end, Ethel and I both won—we got our Mitch, who has made us proud throughout his life. Graduated from high school and college with honors. Star of his university football team. Became a Navy SEAL. A war vet. Landed a top job at a big corporation in New York City. He's a good man. And now he's about to marry you. I for one couldn't be happier, Lisa. I always wanted a daughter, you know? And as far as I'm considered, a daughter-in-law is the next best thing."

"Can I give you a hug?" I asked.

"Thought you'd never ask," he said with a smile.

13

WHEN I RETURNED to the house, I found Ethel sitting in the kitchen on her padded bench next to the bay window. She was wearing a pale-blue apron, her legs were stretched out in front of her, and in her hands was the second novel I'd published with Wenn, *The Dead Shall Rise*.

She's already finished You Only Die Twice? I thought incredulously. *Just how fast does this woman read? She must have finished it while I was with Harold, Mable, Nico, and the boys, because there it is lying next to her. And what's going through her mind now that she's finished it? She's probably wishing that I'd just die once, never mind twice—and preferably before the wedding.*

"Well, hello!" she said, looking up at me over my book. "How was your walk? Did you see get some fresh air? Did you see Harold?"

"I did," I said. "And I saw more than just Harold."

"What does that mean?"

"I saw Mable give birth."

"Mable?" she said with alarm in her voice. "Who is

Mable, and why has she given birth to her child on my property?"

"She's one of your cows," I said.

"Oh," she said. "Harold has names for a few of his favorites. I don't spend much time in the barns anymore, so I don't know of a Mable." Her eyes widened at me. "But *that* must have been something for you to see."

"It was amazing," I said. "I've never witnessed anything like it."

She genuflected when I said that. "Bearing witness to something as sacred and miraculous as the start of a new life can be humbling, can't it?" Ethel said as she tapped her finger against the back of my book. "Especially when they've been denied a life."

Please don't start with me, I thought. *Not now. Let's just get on with the day.*

But she didn't start. Instead, she put the book down on the window sill and stood, smoothing down her apron as she did so. "You know, giving birth to Mitchell stands as the best day of my life," she said. "Marrying Harold comes a close second, of course. But going through the pain of childbirth and then having the rewards of holding Mitchell in my arms for the first time? And then hearing my doctor assure me that he was healthy? No moment in my life has ever been as powerful as that moment, Lisa."

When her eyes suddenly became bright at the thought of giving birth to Tank, she quickly blinked the tears away and apologized to me in embarrassment. Seeing her like this, I knew her connection to Tank was more formidable than I'd ever imagined—and frankly, for good reason.

But what does that mean for us going forward?

"Sorry," she said. "Whenever I think back to that time, I get emotional. I apologize. That's unlike me."

"There's no need to apologize," I said.

"Anyway," she said with a brisk shake of her head. "How about if we cook? Let's make Mitchell's favorite dish of all time—his grandmother's God-given chicken pot pie. I'll walk you through all of it, and then you'll be able to make it for him yourself when you two are...well, you know —married."

"I'm game," I said, ignoring the hesitation in her voice. "But please don't expect much from me, Ethel. There were a few times when my mother tried to show me how to cook, but she and Dad were so busy, I'm afraid it wasn't enough to stick."

"I understand that, but that doesn't mean that *I* can't show you how to cook. On the counter is an apron for you. Put it on, and I'll get the chicken breasts from the refrigerator. Do you see the sheet pan on the island?"

"I do," I said as I slipped my apron over my head.

"And the bottle of olive oil next to it? And the salt and the pepper?"

"I see them."

She closed the refrigerator door, moved beside me, and placed a package of six chicken breasts on the island. "The chicken, salt, pepper, and olive oil alone are all you need to make a delicious meal. Add a salad or some roasted potatoes, and you've got yourself a winner. It's so easy, even a fool could do it."

Was I the fool? I wasn't sure. I seriously didn't know where I stood with her after last night. And since she refused to talk about it, I'd likely never know, which meant that I was left to interrupt every single thing she said to me, especially if it sounded like a slight.

And *that* just had.

"But we're going beyond serving mere chicken breasts

today, so listen closely for the best results. What I need you to remember is that when you make this recipe, the chicken must be cooked on the bone. Never use boneless filets, because if you do, the chicken tends to be dry instead of succulent. Trust me on that. The meat's connection to the bone makes all the difference."

"Good to know," I said. "Should I be writing this down?"

"No need. I e-mailed you the recipe when you left for your walk."

"I see," I said. "Thank you."

"You're welcome. Now, here...take the chicken, assemble the breasts on the pan, pour some olive oil over the skin, and give each breast a good shake of salt and pepper—but not enough to overwhelm."

I did as I was told.

"Perfect," she said, grabbing the pan and putting it into the oven. "These will roast for about thirty-five minutes at three-fifty. Why such a low heat? Because protein always cooks best at a low heat, Lisa. Like the eggs I cooked for you this morning. I cooked them over the lowest heat possible so that they wouldn't be tough. It's these kinds of tips that will make you an accomplished cook."

"Thank you."

"While the chicken roasts, let's chop the vegetables, make the gravy, and then get to what many believe is the hardest part—making the pastry itself. I've already told you that my method is so simple that anyone can master it. Even you."

Even me? Bitch, what are you doing right now?

Instead of reacting, I started chopping carrots, onions, and parsley while she looked over my shoulder, saying noth-ing. When I was finished, Ethel simply nodded her head in approval and then showed me how to make the gravy, to which we added the chopped vegetables and a bag of frozen peas.

"Never think twice about using frozen peas," she said.

"Why's that?"

"Because they are just as good as shucked peas. Trust me, I've tried it, and there is zero difference. Consider that a time saver."

"Noted," I said.

"Can you smell the chicken?" she asked.

"I can."

"It smells delicious, doesn't it?"

"It smells better than the chicken *I* cook." And that was the truth.

"It's all about the heat," she said. "What temperature do you cook your chicken?"

"Four hundred?"

"Then you're about to see the difference a mere fifty degrees can make. Just you wait. Now, trust me here— Mitchell needs you to make this meal for him, especially in the winter. I can't even imagine how much he's missed it— and that he's gone more than a year without having it even once. But we're about to fix that now, aren't we? By the time we're finished, you will have mastered this dish."

And if I don't, what then?

"I'm sure I will," I said.

"Good. Now for the pastry," she said. "My mother's recipe is excellent, but when I saw that fat Contessa woman make her version on television, I decided that since she was literally heaving, sighing, and mooning over it, I probably should give it a shot. And guess what? It was triumphant, as you'd guess just by looking at that woman. I mean, consider how many pastries she must have eaten to turn into the person she's become today. By the looks of her, I'd say she eats whole sticks of butter, bacon grease, and fried whatnots all day long. But I digress. Because I'll give *this* to her—that woman knows what she's doing."

"That's so charitable of you," I said.

"Isn't it? I mean, when a woman lets herself go the way she has, shame on her, I say, because her husband deserves better than that, doesn't he? Not that I think you'll ever have any issues with your weight. What size are you, anyway?"

"I'm a size zero."

"A size what?"

"Zero."

"But that would mean that you don't exist. That would mean that you're not even here with me now."

Don't get your hopes up, old girl.

But then she just pointed a finger at me. "Oh, I see," she said. "You're talking about the world of *high fashion*, aren't you? You're talking *haute couture*. I mean, where else in the world could you be reduced to nothing but zero than in *that* world? In *my* world, I'd say you're probably a size two. Maybe smaller. But a zero? A zero doesn't exist at Macys, Lisa, which is where I do most of my shopping."

"Did you buy your Louis bag there?" I asked with a smile.

"Goodness no! That was a treat! But enough of this talk about fashion. To make the pastry, we now turn to the magic of the food processor. Are you familiar with what it does?"

"I believe it processes food."

Her eyes narrowed in the face of my sarcasm, but then she seemed to catch herself, and in a flash, her features returned to normal.

"So clever," she said. "And always so quick! You know, it's in that way only that you remind me of Tank's first girlfriend, Linda, who also has a quick wit. We've remained friends to this day. We both belong to the same quilting club. We do some shopping here and there, and we have lunch at least once a month. Things like that. Wonderful girl. But she and Mitchell met too early in life for anything serious to happen between them, like marriage and children. I sometimes wonder what would have happened between them if they'd only met later on."

"I guess we'll never find out," I said.

"No," she said wistfully. "Probably not." She arched an eyebrow at me. "Hand me the flour? And the salt and the sugar?"

I slid them toward her.

"Now, pay close attention to what happens next," she said as she added the three ingredients into the processor's bowl, which was fitted with a steel blade. "Because if you don't, this whole experiment of ours could blow up in our faces."

"You're referring to the dough?" I asked.

"Well, of course," she said without looking at me. "I mean...what else?"

AFTER THE DOUGH had rested in the refrigerator for thirty minutes—during which Ethel returned to my novel while I used my SlimPhone to check e-mail and texts and to flick through my Facebook feed—we finished the rest of the recipe.

"Touch the breasts," she said to me as she put the sheet pan of cooled chicken in front of me.

"You want me to touch the breasts?"

"Well, of course. I do—and for good reason. Touch

them. Press a finger against them. If the flesh gives, they aren't fully cooked. But if they're firm, they're ready to go."

I did as I was asked.

"Do they give?" she asked.

"They don't."

"Perfect. That's how you know the breasts are done."

We moved onward, removing the chicken from the bone, slicing the meat into one-inch cubes, and then joining the chicken with the vegetable-and-gravy mixture before we divided all of it between three ovenproof bowls. When we were finished, we covered each bowl with eight-inch rounds of pastry, and then Ethel asked me to brush the tops of them with an egg wash so they would become "a lovely, shimmering, golden brown."

"You did well," she said as she took a butcher knife and started to aggressively stab holes into the tops of the dough. "I think you've got this." Stab, stab, stab. "I *really* do."

"Thank you," I said.

"My pleasure." She put down the knife and clapped her hands. "So!" she said, removing her apron. "How about if we let these rest on the counter for an hour or so before we put them in the oven? They'll take about an hour to bake, and by that time, it will be dinner. But while we wait, we shouldn't waste time. Let's go outside and start to make some decisions."

"Like what?"

"You know, where the tents will go. How you want the flowers arranged and displayed in the gazebo and elsewhere. That sort of thing. We only have a few days left to pull this wedding together, Lisa. Since Harold is going to have the boys set up the tents as well as the propane-fueled air conditioners that will be attached to each of them, I think we should scout out where we want to place those tents, if only so they can be constructed sooner rather than later. Unless anything has changed, it's my understanding there will be three tents, correct?"

"Yes," I said.

"One close to the house for the rehearsal dinner and two near the gazebo?"

"That's right."

"The two tents near the gazebo will be divided between Mitchell and his groomsmen and you and your bridesmaids? Mitchell and you want them air conditioned so you don't have to worry about the heat. Is that still the case?"

"It is."

"Then, let's get to work," she said. "Because I can tell you this, Lisa—now that you're settled in, there is a lot to do—and the next few days are going to go by in a blur!"

14

ETHEL WAS RIGHT—THE next several days did pass in a blur as she and I joined uneasy forces to prepare for my wedding to Tank.

Over the course of the next three days, we took to our to-do list and tended to as much of it as possible so that when Tank arrived, we'd be able to relax and spend time with him. If only because there was so much to be done, each of us became so laser focused on the tasks at hand that we didn't argue once.

We agreed on the placement of the three tents, we went to the caterer to make sure that everything was set for the rehearsal dinner, and the next day, we went to the florist to choose a host of flower arrangements for the wedding, including my bridal bouquet. Since Ethel was severely allergic to several kinds of flowers, we worked our way through what she could tolerate—and what she couldn't—and came to a successful end.

On the third day, the one hundred white chairs we'd requested from a local catering company were delivered and placed in front of the gazebo. A wide red carpet would eventually divide the chairs and lead to the gazebo's steps. As Ethel and I supervised the best way to position the chairs, propane-powered air-conditioning units were being set up outside the tents to blow cool air into them, which was a must as it was so hot here.

When we were finished, Ethel and I visited the woman in charge of making the wedding cake. At first I was concerned, because I saw that she baked out of her house and not out of a working storefront, but the moment I was offered a sample of what to expect, I felt relieved.

The cake was delicious. And the baker, Nancy, said she planned to make the cake bright and early on Saturday morning so that it would be as fresh and as perfect as it could be for the wedding.

When we left her, I knew that Tank and I were in excellent hands.

During the evenings, I took to my room after dinner and caught up with Tank, my family, and my friends over the phone. I talked to my parents, who were beyond excited for me and Tank, and who said they couldn't wait to come to meet Ethel and Harold. Because I didn't want to worry them, I simply told them things were going well and that I was eager to see them.

But when I spoke with Tank, Jennifer, and Blackwell, they got the truth from me, and in return, I got their support. With each day that passed before Tank arrived— which was today, thank God—we all agreed that he must have gotten through to his mother, because with the exception of a few passive-aggressive digs from Ethel, we were working well together, and things were indeed moving forward. Frankly, if I were honest with myself, I knew I couldn't have done any of this without Ethel's help, which I'd told her when we had breakfast yesterday morning.

"I appreciate that, Lisa," she'd said. "And you're certainly welcome—but never forget that I'm also doing this for my son. It's his day, too."

Noted, lady, I'd thought at the time. *But let's be clear on this —you insisted on inviting many of your closest friends to our wedding for a specific reason, and that's because this day is apparently also for you. You want your friends to moon over how beautiful everything is. You want people to walk away thinking how well off the McCollisters are, even though my parents, Tank, and I have footed the bill. You want your friends to see your home and its grounds at their very best—and you're about to succeed when it comes to that because of us. But please don't think for a moment that I don't know you're just working for Tank and me, because I know otherwise. I see through you, Ethel. And this wedding? I already know you are going to make sure that everyone knows it has your name written all over it.*

Unless I could somehow intervene...

"Lovely day," Ethel said to me as we left the house, stepped into her beast of a Navigator, and pulled out of the driveway to pick up Tank at the airport, which had me tingling with anticipation because I was so desperate to see him again.

"I'm beginning to think it's always lovely here," I said. "I mean, every day since I've been here, the sun has been shining. Back in the Northeast where I was raised, it was much more of a mix—to the point that we pretty much called spring mud season. It was that wet—and that awful."

"Here in Nebraska, we long for that kind of mix," she said as we took off down the road. "If you are on a well, as we are, water can sometimes be scarce here. Yes, when the occasional thunderstorm or twister rips through our neck of the woods, we get hammered with rain. But not often enough to saturate the land. Instead, because it's so dry here, the rain just runs off and causes floods."

Always the downer in the room...

"Well, it's still beautiful," I said.

"I'm glad you like it here, Lisa. Perhaps after this week, you and Tank will visit more often. Because goodness knows, his father and I aren't getting any younger. I'd hate to think you'd keep our son from us."

"I'm sorry?" I said.

"That you'd decide it wasn't worth the time to make frequent visits. Because you must know by now that we'd always welcome a visit from both of you. And if on the off chance you couldn't come due to your writing deadlines and obligations with your, um, writing career, I hope you'd allow Mitchell to come alone. Because we do miss him."

"Ethel, just so we are clear—Tank is his own man, and he makes his own decisions. I've never kept him from you."

"But haven't you?"

"No, I haven't. We didn't come this past Christmas due to other obligations. But here we are now, about to be married at your home. That has to mean something."

"I wonder if it does."

"What does that mean?"

"From what I understand, you had no choice but to get married here."

"That isn't true. I could have gotten married at my parents' home."

"You mean at their 'motel'?"

"Yes—their home sits on the property. And it's a lovely house surrounded by beautiful grounds. But my parents are so busy running it during the summer months, I didn't want to ask them to stop everything in an effort to host our wedding, even though I knew they would have done it in a minute if I'd asked them. But I didn't. My parents aren't wealthy, Ethel. What you need to understand is that the income from the motel alone is the reason they're able to eat and pay their bills. When Tank suggested we could get married here, I was grateful for the idea."

"And we took you in," she said as she drove. "We opened our arms and our home to you. For the past several days, I've worked tirelessly at your side."

"And I appreciate that," I said. "But I see where this is going, so before this conversation goes off the rails and one of us says something we'll only come to regret, I suggest you recognize that I did have another option, that I chose not to use it, and that I'd never keep Tank from you. Are we clear?"

"I suppose," she sighed. "Enough talking for now. In the glove box is a new audiobook I'd like to listen to. Would you grab it for me? It's called *Pigs in the Parlor*, and I chose it with you in mind."

Oh, no you didn't.

"*Pigs in the Parlor*?" I said. "Really, Ethel? And you chose it with me in mind?"

"After finishing all of your books, yes, I did choose it with you in mind. Not because of the title but because of the content. Read the description for yourself. Because I am concerned about you, Lisa."

"What's to be concerned about?"

"The reasons are addressed in the book."

I'm not going to let you get to me, Ethel. It's just not happening—not today. Not when I'm about to see Tank. I need to rise way above the bullshit you're serving me right now and act like none of this is touching me.

And so I removed the CD from the glove box and read the description aloud. "'In *Pigs in the Parlor*, Frank

Hammond explains the practical application of the ministry of deliverance, patterned after the ministry of Jesus Christ. He presents information on such topics as: How demons enter, when deliverance is needed, the seven steps in receiving and ministering deliverance, the seven steps in maintaining deliverance, demon manifestations, and practical advice for the deliverance minister. The Hammonds also present a categorized list of fifty-three demonic groupings, including various behavior patterns and addictions.'"

Stunned, I just turned to her. "Do you honestly believe that I have a demonic manifestation?"

"I'm not sure."

"And what's *that* supposed to mean?"

"I'm conflicted."

"How are you conflicted?"

"Because of the things you write and the ease with which you write them. And because you write them so convincingly, I have to believe there must be a reason for it. That you've somehow *experienced* some of the things you've written about in order to be so detailed about all of it."

"Like eating someone's brains?"

She didn't answer, and because she didn't, I wasn't sure whether to laugh in her face—or punch her in the face.

"Do you even know the definition of a demonic manifestation, Ethel? Because I do. I've researched it for my books."

"Of course I know what it means," she said.

"You do?" I said incredulously. "Are you sure?"

"I said that I do."

"Fine." I pulled my SlimPhone out of my handbag and switched it on. "Then, if you do know, let me underscore just how offensive you're being by giving you a proper definition of it." I pressed a button on my cell and said, "Glo, what is the definition of *demonic manifestation*?"

"Let me check on that," Glo said. "OK! Here's what I found about *demonic manifestation* on the web. Traits: foul body odors, hearing animals speak, levitation or astral projection, snarling or growling with hatefulness or viciousness, eyes rolling back in the sockets, evil speech, hearing voices, and foaming at the mouth. Would you like to hear more, Lisa?"

"I would," I said.

"Well, I wouldn't," Ethel said, stiffening in the seat next to me.

But Glo didn't give a damn about what Ethel wanted to hear—she just kept talking.

"OK!" Glo continued in a voice so bright and cheerful that it had no place in this vehicle. "Here are additional traits of demonic manifestation: drooling from the mouth; barking or hissing uninhibitedly; bursts of increased and violent strength; taking joy and satisfaction at another person's tragedy; flittering, wagging, or sticking out of the tongue; continual torment; and patterns of shrill, overbearing and annoying laughter—"

"That's enough," Ethel said.

"It is enough," I agreed, shutting off my phone. "You just crossed another line with me, and you did it deliberately, so I have to wonder—why do you continue to push my buttons? What kind of sick pleasure do you get out of it? And why do you believe that I'm forever going to allow you to do this to me? Because I won't. My patience with you has met its end."

"I'm trying to save you from *you*!" she said.

"I'm sorry—from what?"

"From yourself! For my son!"

"We don't want or need your help. But I will tell you this, Ethel—if I have to use my backup plan, I will."

When I said that, she shot me a seriously freaked-out sidelong glance.

"What backup plan?"

"Two days ago, I called a church just outside Prairie Home. I told them about the situation I was in, and they agreed that if things went sour between us and I needed them, Tank and I could get married there on Saturday."

"Who did you talk to about this? Which church? I'm *known* in this town! That kind of gossip will travel! Oh, my sweet, dear Jesus—it will turn me into the town's newest Beatrice Kaiser!"

"It's none of your business who I spoke to," I said. "But here's your takeaway, Ethel: I *am* getting married to Tank— either at your home or at that church. Obviously, you'll be invited to the former if *that* ever sees the light of day, but if you keep judging me and pressing me, you will never, ever be invited to the latter. Tank called you out on this days ago, and already you're slipping back into how you really feel about me and our wedding. I'm here to tell you that I won't stand for it. If you don't get in line and start treating me with respect, I will cancel our wedding at your home, and Tank and I will get married elsewhere with our friends and family surrounding us. You already know that your son will support whatever decision I make. So, my best advice to you is for you to stop fucking with me. Because if you don't, I plan on playing my final hand—and you'll be out of this wedding for good."

∽

DESPITE THE BLISTERING SUN, the walk to the airport was icy. After Ethel parked the Navigator and we got out of the car, she led the way at a crisp, determined clip, and I stayed several paces behind as we walked into the terminal and moved toward Tank's arrival gate. This was a small regional airport with only six gates, and as I looked around, I saw perhaps a hundred or so people either waiting for a flight or waiting to pick up their loved ones.

But Ethel and I would have to wait to pick up ours. When we stopped to look at the arrivals board, we saw that Tank's plane had been delayed by thirty minutes.

While I took a seat, Ethel walked over to the wall of windows overlooking the tarmac and just stood there, her loathing of me palpable. Had I been too harsh on her? Not at all. I knew from my youth that the only way to shut down a bully was to stand up to one. Everyone had a personal breaking point, and if bullies crossed it, you needed to be prepared to take them on if they did.

And so I had.

After her *Pigs in the Parlor* routine, Ethel had essentially jumped me with both fists swinging. If I regretted anything, it was using the F-bomb on her, if only because I knew she'd eventually use it against me, claiming it a blatant show of disrespect against a Christian woman.

There's nothing I can do at this point, I thought. *Best to get it out of my head.*

And so I did.

Moments before Tank was scheduled to arrive, Ethel came over to me.

"May I sit down?" she asked.

"If you'd like."

Instead of taking the seat next to me, she dropped her Louis down upon it and sat down on the chair next to it.

"Mitchell is going to sense the tension between us the moment he gets off that plane," she said.

"You're right," I said. "He is."

"And he's going to question it."

"You're right," I repeated. "He is."

"So, now you're going to shut down on me?" she asked. "Is that it? You're not going to even talk to me?"

I looked at her and saw the nervous tension on her face, but I didn't give a damn about what she was feeling. She'd been too cruel to me for me to care, gone too far for me to give a shit. I'd officially reached my limit with her.

"I've already made myself clear," I said. "But in case you've suddenly gone deaf, allow me to reiterate what I said to you in the car. You intentionally set me up on the drive over here. You ambushed me with that CD, you insulted me with it, just as you did with the first CD, and the more I sit here thinking about what you've done in the past and how you continue to treat me now, the more I'm considering getting married at that church. Screw your house, Ethel. Tank and I don't need it."

"I need to see my son get married. You will not deny me that."

"It's *my* wedding, Ethel. Tank knows everything. And I can do whatever the hell I want."

"Not when I talk to him. I know the man I gave birth to, Lisa, and he won't stand for any of this. I know it in my *soul* that he won't. After I get done with him, all he's going to see is who you really are as a person."

"That's the thing, Ethel," I said to her in a calm, confident voice. "That's what you don't seem to get. Tank does see me for who I am, and he loves me for it. Just as much as I love him."

Across from us, one of the employees standing at the gate opened its door, signifying that Tank's plane had arrived.

"He's here," I said.

"Please be reasonable," she said in panicky desperation. "If I'm not invited to that wedding, Harold won't go. Think of what that will do to him. What *you* will do to him!"

And that's where she got me, because I did love her husband. And I knew Ethel was right. If I did try to keep her out, I'd also be cheating Harold out of seeing his son get married, which I couldn't do.

Fuck! I thought. *She's right. I can't do that to Harold...or to Tank.*

I might have felt defeated when I stood up, but I nevertheless managed to keep my cool when I looked at her with a stoic face. "If you love your son, I suggest you get yourself together. You're a good actress, Ethel, so put on your best face for Tank now. Because after what he's been through after his friend's death and funeral, he's going to need each of us to support him now."

"I don't need any directions when it comes to you, girl."

"And you're in over your head, Ethel. You know that as well as I do. Right now, *I'm* holding the cards. What you need to think about is whether I'm going to deal you in when it comes to our wedding."

When Tank came through the door and clocked me with a broad smile, my eyes lit up, and my anger immediately cooled. In a rush, I ran over to him, threw myself into his arms, and told him that I loved him as he said the same to me. When he lifted me into the air and started to twirl me around and around while he kissed me on the lips and on my neck, I caught glimpses of Ethel staring at us—and trying to compose herself in the sheer horror of it all.

15

WHEN WE RETURNED to Prairie Home, Harold was there in the driveway to greet us as Ethel maneuvered the Navigator beneath the portico.

"We're home!" she exclaimed. "And there's your father, Mitchell. He's going to be so happy to see you."

On the drive from the airport, Tank and I had chosen to sit in the Navigator's back seat so we could be next to one another. He and his mother exchanged small talk, but I had said very little, and I had to wonder if Tank could sense the tension between us.

"It's good to be home," he said.

"Isn't it?" she said.

As we got out of the vehicle and I saw the happy look on Harold's face as he shook his son's hand before they gave each other a firm slap on the back, I knew in that moment that I had no choice but to get married here. I couldn't deny Harold the pleasure of seeing his son get married—they were too close. They meant too much to each other. And frankly, as much as I couldn't stand Ethel, I knew that if I prevented his own mother from witnessing her son's wedding, there was a good chance I might come to regret it one day.

So, what was I to do now? Tell Tank what she'd done to me today? Ruin the mood before the wedding? Or conceal everything from Tank to prevent that from happening? I was so conflicted that I didn't know what to do, especially since I never concealed anything from Tank.

Just wait and see how this goes...

"Look at the tent!" Ethel said gleefully as she moved in front of the car and put her hand against Tank's back. "That's the one for the rehearsal dinner. Isn't it grand? And look at how close it is to the house. It has air-conditioning, lighting, seating, tables—everything! The other two are down by the gazebo, which you must see. Lisa and I have worked tirelessly together to make everything just right, and your father and a few of the boys have helped as well."

"It's great," Tank said. "Thank you."

"You must see the gazebo and the other tents," she said. "How about if all of us go down and have a look at them? We can take your bags up to your room when we get back."

"You mean 'our' room, right?" Tank said.

"Oh, come on," she said. "It's just two days before your wedding. Just to build anticipation alone, I was thinking that you'd each have separate rooms before you got married."

"Thanks for the thought, but I'll be sleeping with Lisa tonight. We've been living together for a couple of years, Mom. I'm pretty sure you know that we don't have separate bedrooms."

"Whatever you wish," she said with a grim look on her face that she quickly brightened. "So, let's all go down to the gazebo so you can see for yourself where Lisa and you will marry."

"Actually, if you don't mind, I'd like to see it with Lisa alone."

"Why?" Ethel asked.

"Because I haven't seen Lisa in days, and I'd like to spend some time with her."

"But you haven't seen your father and me in over a year."

"Ethel..." Harold said with a warning tone.

"Well, it's true," she said. "And I'd like to see Mitchell's reaction myself."

"You've seen me look surprised and happy before," Tank said as he leaned forward and gave his mother a kiss on the cheek. "Thanks for understanding."

He reached for my hand.

"We might be a while," he said. "Don't come checking up on us, OK?"

"Well, that sounds mysterious," Ethel said. "How long will you be gone?"

"I don't know—we'll be back by...three?"

"But that's three *hours* from now. Just to see the gazebo?"

"And to talk. And to be alone. We'll see you and Dad soon," he said.

"Well, then," she said, looking vaguely panicky at me. Tank or Harold could interpret her look however they wanted, but I knew the reason behind her panic—with Tank and me alone, she knew there was a very good chance I might tell him everything that had transpired between us today. "I guess we'll see you in a couple of hours."

"Three hours," he said.

"Of course." She looked at me with a forced smile. "Lisa, since I can't be there to do it on my own, please show Tank all the efforts we've made to make certain this wedding is perfect. Because with all of your New York friends arriving tomorrow, if things aren't just right, we still have time to make them perfect. There can be no margin of error when it comes to this wedding," she said. "Not on my watch!"

~

"WHAT'S UP WITH MY MOTHER?" Tank asked when we were far enough away from them that they couldn't hear us. "She's acting strange."

"Probably stress," I said.

"Stress from the wedding?"

"Oh, she's definitely stressed out about the wedding."

"How stressed?"

"Really stressed."

"How about you?"

Angry and overwhelmed?

"I'm OK."

"Just OK?" he asked. He put his arm around my shoulders as we walked down the path that led to the gazebo. He drew me in close to him and bent down to kiss me on the mouth, and then we just stopped and held each other. "If there are still things to do, I'm here now and can help, Lisa."

"No, we're good. Everything's set to go. And everyone's excited to come tomorrow. Even Blackwell, although I have a feeling she isn't going to know what to do with herself on a farm. I mean, Bergdorf isn't exactly nearby, is it? So, there's that. I told her to bring a pair of flats, but she refused. She has no idea what she's getting into."

"Actually, that could be kind of fun to watch," he said as we parted and continued down the path.

"Or a total disaster. And then there's Epifania. God only knows what she's going to bring to the table—although I'm secretly dying to see what that is, because you know that shit's going to be good. But do you know who's really going to love it here?"

"That's easy," he said. "Alexa."

"I've already marked out several trees for her to hug."

As we continued to walk forward in silence, I felt Tank grip my hand.

"Well," he said as a hummingbird whizzed past us and hovered above a gathering of pink wildflowers to my right, "that was interesting."

"The bird?"

"No. What I'm referring to is that my mother was behaving like a manic wreck back there, and you don't want to talk about it. So, what's the deal? Because I know you, Lisa. And I know my mother. There's a reason you were silent on the drive from the airport. And there's also a reason why my mother didn't want us to come see the gazebo alone. So, what's the reason?"

"Tank..."

"We tell each other everything, Lisa. We always have. And we can't stop doing that now."

"It's not that I want to stop. It's just that sometimes I'm not sure it's even worth going there."

"What isn't worth going there?"

Oh, Christ...

"If I tell you, it will only upset you, which I don't want to do. What you need to know is that I've handled the situation."

And failed completely.

"What situation? I assume it has to do with my mother. Did she start up with you again? She did, didn't she—even when I warned her not to?"

I looked up at him. "Do you really want to know? Because if I tell you, you're just going to get angry."

"I'm a master at anger management, Lisa. Tell me what happened."

There was no getting around this now. So, despite the ramifications of what might come in the wake of this, I told him everything that had happened between his mother and me today. The full lot of it.

"*Pigs in a Parlor*?" he said to me. "Tell me that's a joke."

"I wish it were. Apparently, after reading my books, your mother has come to the conclusion that I might have a demonic manifestation."

"A demonic manifestation?"

"Oh, you know, that I might be capable of all sorts of evil because my spirit has been overcome by the devil. In case you're wondering what that means, allow me to tell you. At any point, I could hear animals speak, I could levitate or astral-project, I might snarl and growl with hatefulness or viciousness, my eyes might roll back in their sockets, and at any moment, I might foam at the mouth. And that's just part of it, because there's a shitload more."

"She made you listen to that CD?"

"She tried her best, but I refused to listen to it. We had an argument, and I let her have it. What you also need to know is what she's going to tell you the moment she gets you alone."

"And what's that?"

"Two days ago, fearing that something might go wrong between your mother and me again, I secured a church for us just outside of town. We can get married there on Saturday if we want—the church has nothing scheduled, and they'd welcome us and our friends. I told your mother that if she continues to belittle me and humiliate me, we would get married there and not here. And that she won't be invited."

"I agree," he said. "I already told her that would happen if she didn't back off."

"But here's the thing—that might have sounded like a good idea at the time, but we have no choice but to get married here."

He furrowed his brow at me. "Why? We can do whatever the hell we want. Fuck the tents. Fuck the gazebo. This is our wedding, for Christ's sake. If she isn't onboard, I don't want her there."

"But your father *is* onboard, Tank. He's been wonderful to me since I got here. He's had my back in ways you can't even imagine. And because of that alone, I can't deny him the joy of seeing his son get married. Because he *wants* to see you get married. He shouldn't be punished because of his wife's disapproval of me. If we go to that church and Ethel isn't invited, whose side do you think your father will take?"

"My mother's," he said. "He rarely crosses her."

"Then it's done," I said. "Regardless what your mother thinks of me, we get married here, because I can't leave your father out of this. He's been my sole ally while you were gone. And because of that—and especially because I know how much you mean to him and how much he means to you—we'll continue forward as planned. Your mother will think she's won a major victory over me, but to hell with it. I'm not going to allow our issues to ruin this for you and your father."

"You know she's only going to continue to goad you, Lisa—especially when I'm not around."

"And I'm prepared for that," I said. "I just hope you'll support me if I feel she's gone too far and that I need to stand up to her."

"You've got my full support," he said, and then he shook

his head. "My mother is seriously fucked up. I just wish I knew why."

Since I couldn't tell him why, I didn't, because I'd promised Harold I'd never betray him when he'd confided Ethel's past to me. And if one day Tank somehow found out that I'd known before he did, I also knew he would respect me for keeping his father's secret. He wouldn't see it as an act of betrayal. Instead, he'd see it as an act of honor.

For several minutes, we kept walking in silence until the gazebo, the tents, and all the white chairs came into view.

"Look," I said. "There's the gazebo."

"It looks so small from here."

"Trust me, it's huge."

As we came upon it, Tank walked around it, marveling at it. "It's better than it looked in the photos we were sent. It's perfect."

"You should know that your mother personally took charge of the landscaping," I said. "Before I even got here, she saw to every plant, bush, and flower planted around the gazebo. I had nothing to do with it."

"She did all this?"

"Your mother is a complicated woman, Tank, but yes, she did."

"It's amazing," he said as we ascended the steps and stood at the gazebo's center. "And it's also kind of surreal. This is where I'm going to marry you. This is where the rest of our life begins."

I teared up when he said that.

"I can't tell you how long I've waited for this moment," I said. "I'm so happy that it's almost here."

He embraced me when I said that, and then he kissed me. And when he kissed me, the kiss became so heated that Tank eventually swept me into his arms, walked me down the gazebo's steps, and started to move toward one of the tents.

"What are you doing?" I asked.

"Finishing what should have been finished a few days ago," he said in a low voice as he put me down on the grass and parted the entrance to the tent on our right. "You know, when we were interrupted by my mother while we were having phone sex. I've been aching for you ever since." He slapped me on the ass. "Inside."

"But what if your mother comes looking for us?" I said.

"She won't. Inside."

"But I don't trust her. If we do this, it's going to have to be a quickie."

"I don't do quickies."

"You're about to do one now."

"We'll see about that," he said. "Now move. Get naked. I want you."

And I wanted him, so inside we went.

Thankfully, the bottom of each tent had been covered with plastic drop cloths, so at least I wouldn't be walking back to Ethel with grass stains on my hands and knees, my back, or my face. But without the air-conditioning on, it was a sauna in that tent.

"There's no air in here," I said as he started to undress me and I ran my hands along the curve of his ass. "But who cares? God, you feel good. As in *everywhere*. I think I can feel you against my thigh right now."

"You'll be feeling that somewhere else pretty soon. Lift your arms for me."

I lifted them, and suddenly my shirt and bra were gone —which actually felt great, because it allowed my skin to breathe.

"Let me take off your shirt," I said.

"Do it fast."

He was wearing a white polo shirt that was so tight across his broad chest that I couldn't lift it above his head.

"Sorry," I said. "Too tight."

"No problem," he said, ripping it off him. "Ditch the pants."

"Yours or mine?"

"You do yours, and I'll do mine."

I unfastened the top button of my pants and started to remove them. "I'm terrified but weirdly turned on that Ethel might come upon us like this. I mean, just imagine it. The sight of actually seeing us do it instead of just over a phone would probably make her rosary beads melt in her hand."

And then I just stopped when I saw him standing naked and erect in front of me. Tank was so large, muscular, and handsome that he looked like a god to me. "I've missed you," I said. And then I looked down at his crotch. "And I've missed you, as well."

"Lie down on your back," he said.

I did as I was told as Tank knelt down and covered my mouth with a kiss. I hooked my legs around his ass, pulled him closer to me, and felt my body burn with desire as we started to become one.

When our lips parted, Tank lowered his mouth down over one of my breasts. First it was his tongue that teased my nipple, which made me moan in pleasure and surprise before his teeth lightly scored my sensitive flesh, which sent me to gray edges of lust. The jolt of desire I felt at that moment was so consuming that I had to catch my breath— but I was denied the chance when his mouth claimed my other nipple. As he sucked on it, toyed with it, and tasted it, I knew then that he had entered this tent far more seriously than I had. He came here planning to do this—this was the real reason he'd told his parents not to come checking up on us.

He didn't want to wait to make love to me tonight when we retired to our bedroom. He wanted me sooner. He wanted me now.

I looked up at him and saw not only the heat and the desire in his eyes but also the focus and the determination, which was as exciting as it was erotic. He was here to pleasure me in ways he wasn't able to when we were on the phone. He was here to take me away from the past several difficult days since we'd been apart.

With his fingertips now lightly brushing the insides of my outstretched arms, my stomach trembled as I felt warmth radiate through me, finally settling in my core when his fingers drifted down to my rib cage and then lower to my belly as he began to tease my legs open with his touch.

He allowed one finger to brush against my clit, giving me a half smile when my body tensed in response, but he didn't go any further. Instead, he positioned himself so I could feel the full weight of him pulsing against my abdomen before he dipped his head again and allowed his tongue to follow the soft curve of my body until he reared up and his mouth claimed mine again.

Despite how hot it was in the tent, our lovemaking became even hotter. Now dripping with sweat, our skin slick with it, I reached down to grasp him in my hand. I felt the thick weight of his heavy girth, and I wanted him inside me.

But Tank had other plans.

With one swift move, he lifted himself off me and knelt back as he swept me up and into his arms. Somehow, I was suddenly straddling him as his lips met my neck and his arms stroked my back. My breasts, so taut and full, brushed against his chest, sending rivers of ecstasy through me as I pressed them harder against him. Each time his lips connected with my skin, I felt my heartbeat race and the world fall away, this moment becoming more profound because it was just about us.

His giving pleasure to me.

And now my giving pleasure to him.

I released myself from him, knelt before him, and took him into my mouth. I heard him gasp when my tongue met his sensitive skin and felt his body respond with a sharp shiver, and when I started to massage him, taste him, and toy with him, I felt his fingers start to run through the strands of my damp hair as his breathing became more labored.

When he couldn't take it any longer, he positioned me gently onto my back. I saw that his eyes had become hooded with desire, and I watched his head move toward my sex before he claimed it with his mouth and then with his tongue.

He licked me slowly and steadily before the stubble on his chin swept against me. I nearly came when that happened, but Tank didn't stop. If anything, it felt like a blissful eternity before he stopped and finally entered me.

I was so wet that our bodies joined together with surprising ease as Tank began to thrust into me, whispering again and again as he did so that he loved me. I told him the same as I lifted up my hips in an effort to take all of him, which I did. I swung my arms around him, rode him as he drove into me, and then just closed my eyes and allowed him to take me beyond the confines of this tent, beyond the hell that had been Prairie Home, and into an ether that I'd never known before.

Not even with him.

As we made love on the plastic drop cloth, it was with a

mixture of aggression and profound tenderness. And as Tank's eyes met mine, I had to wonder if sex with him would only get better when we were married. Because this? This was beyond anything we'd ever experienced together. As each of us drove the other toward climax, I felt that almost certainly was the case—just I was almost certain that Ethel had likely just heard the cries of our frantic release.

16

"SHE'S GOING TO KNOW," I said to Tank as we lay on our backs beneath the shade of the gazebo's roof. We'd been there for the past thirty minutes, trying to dry off. "I mean, I checked my reflection in the pond, for God's sake—you know, when one of those swans snapped at my forehead. Who knew they were so aggressive?"

"I knew."

"Thanks for telling me."

"I had my back to you when you did that."

"It actually was kind of funny," I said. "For a moment, I thought I was going to fall in. And maybe I should have, because at least then I'd have a good reason for looking the way I do."

He turned his head toward me and reached out to brush my cheek with the back of his index finger. "You don't look bad. In fact, I think you look more beautiful than ever. You've got that glow about you."

"If I'm glowing, it's because I've become a nuclear reactor of nerves. You do realize that she's going to smell the sex on us, don't you?"

"Let her. I don't care—and you shouldn't, either."

"You can say that because she bows down to you. She won't dare cross you. As for me? No such luck."

"Lisa, I think you're underestimating yourself. I fell in love with you because of your strength, your intelligence, and your feistiness. And also because you really know how to make love to your man, which you just showed me in that tent over there."

"Forever to be known as the microwave sex oven."

"It did get kind of hot in there, didn't it?"

"In the best and worst ways."

He sat up, and I followed suit.

"We should go," he said. "We've only been gone two hours now. Let's head back and make her happy that it didn't turn out to be the three hours I'd promised. I don't know about you, but I want to take a shower."

"Same here, but I need something to drink first. I'm thirsty."

"Get yourself something to drink and join me in the shower?"

"Let's not push her too far. You take a shower, I'll grab some iced tea, and then I'll start unpacking your bags while you wash off."

"Just so you know, I plan on taking one mother of a long, cold shower."

"I plan on doing the same when you're finished."

He stood and offered his hand to me. "Let's go," he said, helping me to my feet and putting an arm around my waist as we descended the gazebo's steps. "And don't worry about my mother. If she's in the kitchen when we get there, I'll wait for you to get your glass of iced tea, and then we can go upstairs to our bedroom together. You won't be alone with her, and she won't say a word to you with me there."

"Consider that a deal," I said. "Let's go."

BUT WHEN WE arrived at the house and walked through to the kitchen, Ethel was nowhere to be found. In silence, I looked at Tank, who simply shrugged, put a finger to his lips, and pointed at the refrigerator.

"She's probably working outside in one of her gardens," he said in a quiet voice to me. "Dad's likely in one of the barns. Grab yourself some tea and meet me upstairs."

"I'll be quick," I said. "Scoot."

After he gave me a kiss on the mouth, he left the kitchen, and I heard him race up the stairs to our bedroom. Meanwhile, I pulled a pitcher of iced tea from the fridge, grabbed a tray of ice from the freezer, and popped a few cubes into a glass I took from one of the cupboards over the sink. It was only as I started to pour that I heard Ethel's voice coming from beyond the kitchen, down the hallway that led to the parlor, which was at the other end of the house.

Christ, I thought, not wanting her to catch me looking like this. *Of course she's here. I need to move it.*

But then I just stopped cold when I heard her raise her voice and say, "You're my sister, for goodness' sake, Margaret. You know how hard I've been trying to break this wedding off between them. Apparently I've failed, because this is happening, and now I can officially tell you that you and Stan need to be here tomorrow night for the dinner and Saturday afternoon to witness my only son wed the devil herself."

Trying to break off our wedding? I thought in horror. *She's been trying to break off our fucking wedding? If she's told her sister what she's been trying to do, then how many other people has she poisoned against me? How many friends and family members of hers will be sitting at that gazebo on Saturday knowing what she thinks of me and that she failed to wedge herself between me and her son?*

At that moment, I wasn't sure who I'd just become, because when I heard her say those words, the fireball of rage that scorched through me was apparently enough to make me see red.

And not a good kind of red.

It was the kind of red you'd see on a matador's cape. And right now? Right now, I was the pissed-off bull with several lances planted into my bloodied back who was about to lash out and gore a woman who had been armed with this cruel, unbelievable, nefarious agenda all along.

But as angry and as betrayed as I felt, I knew I needed to be smart about this. I couldn't give myself away. I wanted her to keep talking, not realizing that we'd come back early. And so, I put the pitcher of iced tea down on the countertop, removed my shoes, grabbed my phone from my pants pocket, and started to pad down the hallway that led to the closed library door.

"Where does Harold stand?" I heard her say. "He was chilly toward her when they first met a year or so ago because I demanded he be tough on her given what she writes. But since then? Since all the telephone calls they've had with Mitchell since it was decided they'd get married here? Somehow, he's actually come to *like* her, which I can't fathom for the life of me."

Keep talking, lady. Give me the kindling I need.

"No, you need to understand, Margaret. Harold's never been as sensitive to these things as I've been. He doesn't see the evil I see in her. Did I tell you that I read her books? No? That must have been somebody else, probably Linda, because she's as horrified by all this as I am. Yes, Linda. You remember—Mitchell's first girlfriend. The one I like."

I kept moving forward, trying my best not to reveal myself too soon. For a house this old, it was solid, and the hardwood floor thankfully didn't creak and give me away.

"Anyway, about her books. I read all of them this week right under her own nose. And you cannot believe the filth that's in them. You really can't, because I know it would make your blood run as cold as mine if you even glanced at their covers alone. In our world, only Christ has risen. But in her world? The undead rise again and again! And it gets even worse! In her books, she writes vivid scenes of women having abortions, which are so detailed that I'm certain she's had plenty of them herself, even though when I challenged her on that, she disputed that claim. I call that a lie. I call her whole being a sacrilege! To know that this woman—this *heathen of an unworldly shebeast*—will one day give birth to my grandchildren makes me want to vomit."

My blood pressure spiked when she said that. I loved children. How dare she say such a thing about me?

"But what can I do?" she said. "Nothing. Since I failed to break them up, I'm literally without hope. No—I really am. She's cast some sort of voodoo spell over my son, because I think my Mitchell really does believe he's in love with her. I don't know what else to say or do, because I can tell you this —I've tried everything in my power to end this since the day she arrived here in her fancy private jet. All I'm left to do now is accept defeat and know that the devil has won, as he often does. What's done is done."

I opened the door when she said that, and she whirled around in surprise, looking at me in horror. When she saw my phone, which was pointed straight at her, her jaw dropped.

"The phone is on, Ethel," I said. "I've been recording your conversation with your sister from the hallway, and now I'm recording you on video."

Almost at once, the color drained from her face as it came to her that at least some part of her conversation with her sister was locked away on my phone and that I likely had proof she'd been meddling into my relationship with her son—to the point that she wanted to smash it apart.

"What in the—*put that down!*"

I kicked the door behind me and took a step toward her. "Make me."

"Make you? *Make you?* Do you think I'm going to get *violent* with you?"

"After what I just heard, I wouldn't put anything past you, Ethel. Nothing."

"I asked you to put down the phone. I'm demanding that you do it now."

"How about if you get off the phone, Ethel? Hang up now, and you and I will have a little chat. We'll see if we can come to a deal, and depending on how that goes, I'll leave... and we'll see what happens next."

She moved to speak, but when she saw the steel in my eyes—and that my phone was still trained on her face—she lifted the receiver and said, "Margaret? I'll need to call you back. What's that? Yes, she's in here with me now. I'll see you tomorrow. Or not. I don't know. I'll call you later."

She hung up the phone and looked at me with such bitter hatred in her eyes that the full truth of her loathing of me was revealed not only to me but also to the camera. In an odd way, I was grateful to finally see her unbridled hatred of me, if only so that I'd know in my heart there would be no more guessing when it came to her. No more wondering if we could somehow turn our relationship around after the wedding. Because after what I'd just heard, I knew that could never be the case—that I could never forgive her and that she'd never come to accept me.

But that didn't mean I couldn't win against her in the end.

"Put down the phone now, or I will scream out for my husband," she said.

"Please do," I said. "And please also call out for Tank if you want. Because the rest of your life is right now in your hands, Ethel, especially when it comes to how your husband and your son will view you if I play them this recording. So...decide. Each of them can either hear that you tried to break Tank and me up by trying to get into my head this week, or we can keep your vicious little secret between us. Your choice. Scream now, or shut the fuck up and listen to me."

"How do I even know you're recording me now?" she asked. "That you've recorded anything? You could be lying to me, because that's what you people do best."

At this point, I had more than enough video to get what I wanted from her. So, I pressed the red stop button, held up the phone so that the screen faced her, and played back the entire recording. With an intensity that thrummed between us, Ethel listened to her own voice and then watched with a start as I burst into the room and we began our initial exchange of words. When the video ended, she looked as pale as a ghost.

"If you play that to Mitchell, he'd never forgive me," she said.

"You're right. He wouldn't."

She was visibly trembling, either in rage or in fear—or possibly a combination of both. Then she said, "What do you want from me? Because you obviously want something —I can see it in your eyes."

"What I'd really like to do is slap that smug face of yours so hard that you'd find yourself spitting out a few teeth and coughing up some blood. But since I'm not a particularly violent person, Ethel—despite what you might think of me because of the books I write—I want something else from you in exchange for my keeping this video private."

"And what is that?"

"From this point forward, you will stop interfering in my relationship with your son. That ends now. You also will be civil toward me, as I have tried to be civil toward you ever since I first met you. You will be polite, even if it kills you, because I am officially done with your deranged treatment of me. Either you agree, or I will bring this recording to Tank now and show it to him. But please, know this—if you do agree to my terms and try some shit at a later date, you need to know that I'll show the video to him then. And if you think for one stupid moment that I might accidentally delete the video off my phone or that I might even lose my phone, be advised that all the information I just recorded is already stored in the cloud."

"What cloud?" she asked. "I don't even know what that means."

"I didn't think you would, so let me spell it out for you. Everything on my phone—photos, videos, e-books, you name it—is instantly stored remotely and securely on my hosting company's servers the moment I add something new to my phone. Like this video, for instance. It's already sitting there, waiting for me to access it. If you don't understand that, here's your takeaway, Ethel: if something happens to my phone or if the video somehow becomes corrupted on it, that video is now stored elsewhere in a backup copy that I can retrieve whenever I like. So, down the road, if you are stupid enough to even think of testing me again, always remember that I'll have a copy of that video to show to your son. And if I do that—which I will, because this is your last shot in saving your relationship with Tank—I think we both know you'll never see him again. Are we understood?"

"You'd do that to me, wouldn't you?"

"Without hesitation. I'll do anything to protect my marriage to Tank, especially from the pig that's in the parlor with me now. So, agree or disagree, because I need to get back to Tank."

"Naturally, I agree. What choice do I have?"

"If you want your son in your life, none." I put the phone into my pants pocket and just looked at her. "Be grateful that I'm not taking this to him now, Ethel, because I could have. But I won't, because I want to protect Tank from who is mother really is—unless you give me a serious reason not to. Consider that going forward. You will never do anything to jeopardize our relationship again, you will be polite to me, and I will be polite to you—and even though neither of us will ever mean it, that's still going to be the case."

Before I turned to leave, I clocked her with a glance. "By the way, we will be getting married here. Nothing has changed—as long as you keep up your end of the deal. And...oh!" I said, almost as if it were an afterthought. "If you're wondering why I look like a hot mess right now, it's because when Tank and I were down at the gazebo, he wanted to make love to me, so we defiled one of the tents while we there. And it was wonderful, Ethel. Pure magic. In fact, a part of me wished you could have been there to witness it, if only so you could have seen us making love in person and not on a phone—and also so you could be reminded of what real love is."

~

LATER, after I'd added fresh cubes of ice to my glass of iced tea, I took the stairs to our bedroom, opened the door, and saw Tank getting dressed at the foot of the bed.

"Where have you been?" he asked.

I could never tell him the truth, if only because I never wanted to be the reason why he'd never have a relationship with his mother again—and perhaps even his father, if Harold decided to side with her.

"Your mother caught me," I said. "But it's fine. No questions were asked about my appearance."

That part was true—I'd shared the reasons for it with her myself.

"What did she want?"

"Just wedding stuff," I said, taking my phone out of my pocket, placing it on one of the bedside tables, and starting to remove my clothes. "As in *boring* wedding stuff. Now, move aside, big boy, because this girl needs to take a shower."

"You expect me to just move aside when you're standing naked in front of me like that?"

Knowing in my gut that I had enough on Ethel McCollister to keep her in line for the rest of our lives, I looked mischievously at him.

"I don't know," I said. "Are you sure you got completely washed off? I mean, I know that with those broad shoulders and back of yours alone, it must be hard for you to truly rinse off."

"Are you suggesting I didn't get all the suds off me?"

"I'm more than just suggesting. So...get in the shower with me."

With a wicked smile, Tank tore off his navy-blue polo and slapped me on the ass as I giggled past him toward the shower. And when he joined me there, we made love for a second time that day.

AFTER A PERFECTLY CIVIL dinner with his parents, throughout which Ethel went out of her way to make enthusiastic conversation about all the guests who would arrive tomorrow and the wedding that was to come, I waited for a pause before I excused myself.

"I should call Jennifer," I said to Tank. "They leave in the morning. How about if you continue to catch up with your parents while I step outside and give her a quick call? I won't be long. I just want to make sure everything is good to go before they come."

"You've got it," he said.

Outside, I started to walk down the path that led to the gazebo as I dialed Jennifer's cell. The sun had dipped in the sky, but it was still sunny out, although not nearly as hot. When she answered, hearing her voice was like a balm to me.

"Pour me a martini," I said.

"Consider it poured. What's up, lovecat? Ready for the big day? Or are you stressed out by it, hence the requested martini?"

I told her everything that had transpired between Ethel and me.

"I'm so sorry, Lisa," she said. "What the hell? She seriously tried to do that to you?"

"She did."

"But you of all people don't deserve that kind of treatment. Still, if this is any consolation, good on you for doing what you did. Grabbing your phone was a brilliant move."

"Let's just call it an instinctive one. I think that when I heard her say to her sister that she'd failed to break Tank and me apart, on some unconscious level I knew I needed proof of what was being said, if only so I could use it against her in the future. The mind is a strange thing, Jennifer, and mine went into overdrive."

"Do you think this is under control now?"

"For the moment, yes. For the long term, probably. I think she dug herself into such an ugly hole that she knows if she wants to continue to have a relationship with her son, she needs to just step the fuck back, be polite, and let us be."

"I hope that's the case."

"For Tank's sake, I hope it is. Because if she does go there, I will show him that video, Jennifer. I'll have no other choice, because I can't have that kind of toxicity in our lives. Especially not after we are married."

"I don't blame you."

"Anyway," I said. "Enough of that, because frankly I'm exhausted by it. How are you? Ready to be my matron of honor?"

"Of course!" she said with enthusiasm. "I only wish that *matron of honor* didn't make me sound so goddamned old."

"Sounding old and looking old are two different things."

"True…"

"And you look far from old, so I say you should carry your title with a badge of honor."

"I would have anyway."

"Listen," I said. "I told Tank and his parents that I'd only be a moment, but there's another reason I called."

"What reason?"

"I need you to do something for me."

"Name it."

"It's for tomorrow."

"Why is everything sounding weirdly cryptic right now?"

"It's because what I have in mind might not be so nice."

"What's not so nice?"

I told her.

"Really?" she said. "Did you learn nothing from Michelle Obama? You know, 'When they go low, we go high'?"

"Lovely sentiment but worthless to me now. I need you to listen to me on this."

"OK," she said.

"I want someone to offer them to her tomorrow as a present, and it needs to be done in a very specific way."

"What way?"

I told her. "If it's not done just like that, she'll know, so make sure they're completely covered. Otherwise, if she sees even a hint of them, she'll run from them."

"Are you sure about this? Because if this happens, she could have a major—"

"I *want* it to happen. She *deserves* to have this happen to her."

"Actually, after what you just told me, she kind of does."

"Can you make it happen? It doesn't need to come from you. I mean, maybe someone else could do it."

"Like Blackwell?" she asked. "If you allow me to tell her what she tried to do to you, she'd do it in a hot second. If not her, then Daniella would, that's for sure. She'd totally be up for that kind of evil."

"Will you ask Blackwell first? I'd love it if it came from her."

"I will, but I already know that she'll do it, if only because she's going to be pissed once I tell her *why* you want this done." She paused for a moment. "This could go all sorts of wrong, you know?"

"Not with me in possession of that video!"

"All right. Consider it another wedding gift to you. We'll see you tomorrow at noon, my evil one. Say hello to Tank for us. I love you, doll."

"I love you more," I said.

And then, with a rush of excitement for what was to come tomorrow, I clicked off my phone and walked back to the house.

17

AT ELEVEN THE NEXT MORNING, I was in the bedroom, happily steaming the wrinkles out of my wedding gown, when I received a text from Jennifer saying they'd arrived safely and that they'd soon be on their way.

"Blackwell's armed and dangerous," she said. "Tell me now if you still want to go through with this."

"Absolutely," I texted back, grateful I was alone—Tank was with his father in one of the barns. On one level, I knew what we had in mind for Ethel was wrong, but after hearing her admit she'd been trying for years to break Tank and me up? That was such a major betrayal of her son and me that there was no way I could let off with a mere slap on the wrist. And since I couldn't help myself, we were doing this. "Bring it on."

"We'll be bringing it. And yes, we followed your instructions. See you soon—and gird your loins in the process, because shit's about to get real!"

It is, I thought as I walked over to one of the bedroom windows and opened it so I could hear them when they arrived. *And I'm perfectly fine with whatever happens.*

About thirty minutes later, I'd just finished making sure my dress was perfect when I heard the sound of several cars turning into the driveway.

"Lisa!" I heard Ethel call up to me. "Your friends are here!"

And so they are.

I hurried down the stairs just as Ethel walked briskly into the foyer from the kitchen. In unison, we stopped and gave one another a cool glance.

Today, I noted, Ethel had brought her A game.

Full hair and makeup, which I had to admit was done to perfection, and a pair of beige slacks matched with a stylish, deep-blue jersey top. On her feet were a pair of pretty sandals that not only matched the color of her top but were, as I recognized at once, Christian Louboutins.

She probably bought them because she thought they were made by a Christian, I thought. *I wonder how she'd react if she knew that the man who'd designed her shoes is gay? She'd probably try to pray her shoes away.*

"I've already called down to the barn," she said. "Mitchell and Harold are on their way now."

"Excellent," I said. "In the meantime, let me introduce you to our friends."

"But shouldn't we wait for the boys?"

"And keep our guests waiting?" I said. "That would be rude. We should greet them now."

"Then, after you," she said, motioning toward the door.

Why do I have to go first? So you can plant a knife in my back?

But when I opened the door and saw the three stretch limousines gleaming shiny black in front of the house, I had to stifle a laugh. If Ethel thought she'd seen a glimpse into my life when I'd flown private, she wasn't going to know what to do with herself when she laid eyes on Jennifer and Alex, who pretty much always looked like a couple of movie stars one step away from a red carpet. And then there was Blackwell, who naturally would be decked out in Chanel. And if that weren't enough, Alexa, Daniella, Cutter, Bernie, Epifania, and her beau, Rudman, also were in those cars. Since all of them had just come from the city, I knew for a fact they hadn't left it thinking country chic.

"Well, this is a show," Ethel said as she stood on the porch with me. "I mean, is this even necessary? We're in Prairie Home, Nebraska, for goodness' sake. As I said to you when you chose to fly private, there's no need to impress anyone here, Lisa. We just don't care about these sorts of things."

Then why did you spend nearly a grand on those Louboutins, lady? And four grand on your Louis?

"My friends are well beyond trying to impress anyone, Ethel," I said. "Being driven in limousines is as natural to them as driving your Navigator is to you. You know that Alex is a billionaire. This is just how they live. They aren't trying to impress anyone."

"Well, that's some life they must live," she said. "I hope they donate to charity, especially given *their* kind of money."

"All of them are very generous, especially when it comes to Planned Parenthood," I said with a smile so sugary it was meant to rot her teeth. "I mean, you should see the kind of money all of them funnel into that organization. Tens of millions."

When I shoved that bitter pill down her throat, she moved to speak, but then she caught herself and remained silent. "The drivers are opening their doors," I said. "Let's go and say hello. Look—there's Jennifer and Alex now. Jennifer!" I called as I hurried down the front steps.

"There's the bride-to-be," she said with a big smile.

"You're wearing heels—be careful on the gravel drive."

"I'm fine. Come and give me a hug."

"You look more than fine," I said as I took her into my arms. And that was an understatement. She was wearing a Ralph Lauren Capri striped shirt open at the throat and knotted at the navel, white matchstick jeans, and a pair of Fendi patent-leather T-strap sandals in gold. Her long brown hair shimmered over her shoulders and down her back in thick, loose curls. "You look terrific. I'm so glad you're here. I can't tell you."

I pulled away from her, and for a moment, we just looked at one another.

"Lisa, you're getting married," she said.

"I know—I still can't believe it."

"How has your day been?" she asked in a softer voice.

"So far, so good."

"I can see Ethel out of my peripheral vision..."

"Sorry about that. Can you smite her for me?"

"I would if I could."

"Not good enough."

"Hi," Alex said as he stepped up beside us.

"Good Lord," I said when I turned to him. "Look at you, Mr. Wenn. You look like a stud."

He was wearing jeans, a white T-shirt, and dark aviator sunglasses. I knew Alex was in great physical shape, but I hadn't guessed he was nearly as ripped as this, especially since I generally saw him in a business suit.

"And where did that come from?" he asked.

"You know me—no filter." I gave him a hug and looked at Jennifer over his shoulder. "He needs to dress like this more often. Your stock would spike!"

"You're terrible," she said. "Even though I have to agree."

I heard the others getting out of their cars. Looking up, I saw Blackwell, who arched a single eyebrow at me before she blew me a kiss, and in the car behind her, I watched Epifania step out and into the sun with Rudman right behind her, his hand firmly against her back. When she saw me, she called out to me.

"Look at you, the cookie!" she said. "Thank the Dolly Yama that Epifania is the finally here! Because what if she wasn't? This wedding be a drag, that what!" And then, she suddenly threw up her hands as she looked around the property. "*Heyzeuz Cristo*, the last time I saw something this flat, it was before I had my boobies done!" She took Rudman by the arm and pointed at something in the fields that stretched before them. "Look, my sexy Rudsy, see that bull over there? Since there can only be one bull here while we here, Epifania say you go over and knock it out cold. Because everyone know that you're the real bull! The beeg bull! The hung like the bull!"

Oh, my God...I love her so much I could faint!

I gave Epifania and Rudman an enthusiastic wave before I returned my attention to Jennifer and Alex, who were trying their best to keep their expressions neutral. "Don't you dare laugh," I said to them in a low voice.

"It's not easy," Alex said.

"We're trying our best to keep it together," Jennifer said.

"Try harder."

"With Epifania here, you already know you're asking the impossible."

"True," I said. "And noted." I lowered my voice. "Now, let me introduce you to Tank's mother, because that's a surefire way to welcome you fully into the dark reaches of my bleaker-than-bleak world."

"Where is Tank?" Alex asked. "I haven't seen him yet."

"He and his father should be here shortly—they were down working in one of the barns." I turned to Ethel, who hadn't left the porch and who was now looking down at us with an uncomfortable smile, likely because the loose cannon of Park Avenue—otherwise known as Epifania Zapopa—had just opened her trap in ways that Ethel thought were vulgar. And frankly, if that was the case, I couldn't really blame her, because there was no holding back when it came to the Zapopa.

Not that I cared. My friends were my family—not Ethel.

"Ethel, would you like to meet Alex and Jennifer Wenn?"

"In fact, I would."

As she came down the stairs, Ethel moved with an elegance I'd only seen once in her before. It had been when she'd first picked me up at the airport, which underscored what a fine actress she was. I knew that in her heart she wanted to meet *none* of my friends. Still, with a warm smile, she practically floated toward us as if she were on a cloud being delivered by the baby Jesus himself.

"Hello," she said as she shook their hands. "I'm Ethel McCollister—Mitchell's mother. It's so good to finally meet you."

"We've heard so much about you," Jennifer said. "It's also nice to meet you, Mrs. McCollister."

"Please, it's Ethel. But I'm naturally curious as to what you've heard."

"That you're a terrific cook, for one," Jennifer said, not missing a beat. "And that you made the grounds around the gazebo look beautiful. Lisa told us so. She raved about it."

At that, Ethel blinked.

"She did?"

"She did. She said that you saw to the plantings your-self. She said that what you did for Tank and her is stunning. I can't wait to see it, including the pond and all the swans."

"Neither can I," Alex said.

"Well," Ethel said. "How nice of Lisa. How *kind* of her. She does have a generous heart, doesn't she?"

After the deal I struck with you yesterday, lady, you'd better believe I do!

"Hey!" I heard Tank call out behind me. "Look who's here!"

"Everyone's here," I said, turning to see him and Harold walking toward us. "Well, everyone from Manhattan, that is. Still more to come as the day goes on, including my parents, whom I can't wait to see."

"Oh!" Ethel said as she looked at Tank and Harold. "Just look at the mess you've made of yourselves! You look as if you've been rolling around in the hay, for goodness' sake, while our guests look as if they've just stepped out of any number of fashion magazines!"

"They're our friends, Mom," Tank said to her as he walked toward us. "None of them care what Dad and I look like."

"But still!"

"It's not an issue, so let's not turn it into one."

"Well, I just—"

"Good to see you, buddy," Tank said to Alex as they shook hands and exchanged a quick bro hug. "Ready to have my back tomorrow?"

"Just as you've always had mine."

"Dad, this is Alex Wenn. Alex, this is my father, Harold."

The two men shook hands.

"Good to finally meet you, Alex," Harold said. "Thanks for giving my boy the opportunity of a lifetime."

"Your son is my best friend," Alex said. "He has saved my

life and my wife's life too many times to count. And he was instrumental when it came to saving Lisa's life. Your son is a hero, Harold. I know you don't need me to tell you that, but it's true. I consider him to be the brother I never had."

"Don't make me cry," Tank said.

Alex laughed at that and punched Tank in the arm. But what Alex had said to Tank was real—and I knew that Tank felt the same way toward Alex. After so many years of friendship, they practically *were* brothers.

"This place is kind of like Maine," I heard Daniella say in the distance. "Not a skyscraper in sight, but holy God is there a shitload of grass and trees."

And there goes the mouth on that one...

"What are those over there?" I heard her ask her sister.

"You know exactly what they are, Daniella," Alexa said. "And if you don't, you officially are an idiot."

"I'm joking!" she said. "I know a cow when I see one. But the one Epifania pointed out earlier is different. It looks like that bronze statue on Wall Street."

"That would be a bull," Alexa said. "The rest of them are cows. And you can thank your favorite pair of leather pants for them, because some cow somewhere died for them."

"Everyone dies," Daniella said. "Even you will, Alexa, despite your vegan and pesticide-free lifestyle. So, please save me from your choked-up political rants. What you need to know is that I'm totes down with the cows, because those leather pants of mine are on fire when I wear them. Cutter likes them—don't you, Cutter?"

"I pretty much like anything you wear, Daniella," he said. And then he dipped his head to her ear and dropped his voice so low that I couldn't hear him.

"Right," Daniella said. "Sorry—forgot."

Forgot your tongue? Thank you, Cutter.

"Good afternoon," I heard Blackwell say as she approached us.

"Barbara!" I said.

"It's nice to see you, my darling girl." As expected, Blackwell was decked out to the nines in Chanel, this time in the form of a bright-white suit with black piping. Her hair had recently been colored and cut into a stylish new bob, likely by Bernie. And whether due to a healthy injection of Botox or Bernie's magic with the brush, she looked years younger to me.

"I'm so glad you're here," I said as we embraced.

"Where else would I be, my little scribbler?"

"I don't know—maybe Bergdorf?"

"While I miss it terribly, I wouldn't have missed *this* for the world. Now, while I have your ear and no one else can hear me, are we still going forward with this insidious but absolutely wonderful plan of yours?"

"Hell, yes."

"Well," she said before she parted from me and looked at Ethel. "Then let's get it done."

My stomach clenched when she said that.

"Hello," she said as she walked over and shook Ethel's hand. "Barbara Blackwell. Nice to meet you, Ethel. And also nice to meet you, Harold. I've heard so many good things about each of you."

"That seems to be a recurring theme," Ethel said with a light titter. "My goodness, how Lisa has talked us up, Harold. And even me! I should probably be embarrassed."

Actually, you should be, bitch, because they know all about your manipulative ass.

"It's good to finally meet both of you," Blackwell said. "Your home and the surroundings are divoon."

"They're what?" Ethel said.

"Divoon, darling. Divoon."

"I don't know what that means."

"It means good things, but since it might not translate here, don't trouble yourself with it. Please allow me to introduce you to my daughters, Alexa and Daniella."

"It's good to meet you both," they said in unison when Blackwell urged them forward.

"And it's lovely to meet such lovely girls," Ethel said.

"This is Cutter," Blackwell said. "As you know, he works under Tank at Wenn. What you might not know is that he happens to be smitten with my daughter, Daniella."

"It's a pleasure," Cutter said to both of them as they exchanged handshakes and greetings.

"Everyone is so good looking," Ethel said. "Many of you look like celebrities."

"That's because many of us are," Blackwell said without hesitation, and then she paused for a moment to look around her. "Now for Bernie," she said. "But where is he? Bernie!" she called out. "Bernie, darling, where are you? Bernie! Bernie! How can it be that I can't even see you! Have you run away? Is the country already too much? Oh, look! There you are, still standing beside our limousine. Why are you looking over at the barns? What's captured your attention there? The cows or the cowboys? Doesn't matter, because I already know. Come, meet Tank's parents."

"My pleasure," Bernie said. As he came over to us, I watched him with genuine affection. Bernie was a slender, stylish, good-looking man in his midfifties with a shock of beautifully cut silver hair offset by light-blue eyes. Over the past few years, he'd become one of my very favorite people in the world, especially since he loved to share his stories about his racy past. Like Jennifer, I couldn't get enough of them.

"*Bonjour*," Bernie said to Ethel when they shook hands.

"A pleasure," Ethel said, sizing him up with a swift, critical glance that made me want to shove my fist into her face.

"I'm Harold, Bernie," Harold said as the two men shook hands. "Happy to have you here."

"*Naturellement. Je ne serais nulle part ailleurs*," he said.

"Excuse me?" Ethel said.

"Sorry," he said. "Whenever I see such a vast expanse of land, blue skies, and such fresh air, it naturally reminds me of my time in Provence, and I slip into French."

"How absolutely peculiar," Ethel said. "Is your wife with you, Bernie? Did she come with you?"

"My *what*?"

"Your wife."

"That's a new one," he said. "Very funny, Ethel."

"But I was being serious."

He looked at Ethel for a moment and then turned to Blackwell. "Is she suggesting that I can pass in Nebraska?"

"Maybe for her, my dear," Blackwell said, patting her bob. "But if you stood any closer to *my* suit, I might catch fire."

"Ethel, I don't have a wife," he said to her.

"But you're so handsome—so well dressed. Certainly you have a wife, and one with a good eye for fashion."

"I don't."

"I wonder why that is..."

"I wonder why you wonder. I'm gay, Ethel. There is no wife. Although I do have to say that after looking at some of the men who work on your farm, I see plenty of possibilities for a relationship."

"Well, I'm afraid there won't be any of that," she said.

"We'll see," he said. "You never know. Love is in the air, after all. Anyway, nice to meet you just the same."

"What about me and my Rudsy?" I heard Epifania say. "This heat remind me of all those years I spent on a fucking banana leaf! It's a real killer out here, that for the sure! But I'm not here to the whine and the dine, so! How about if me and my sexy Rudsy say hello to the 'rents and that we all just get the hell inside before we faint from this fucking heat? Because if we do faint? Epifania here to tell you truth—none of that sheet gonna look good on any of us."

"Who exactly is this woman coming toward me," Ethel said to me in horror.

"One of my best friends," I said. "Be nice to her, or she might cast a spell on you."

"She might what?"

"It's a joke. Say hello."

After Epifania and Rudman introduced themselves to Ethel and Harold, I looked over at Blackwell, who caught my glance before she tapped herself on the forehead and said, "Oh...how could I have forgotten?"

"Sorry?" I asked her with a stirring in my gut.

"My present to your future mother-in-law!"

And here we go!

"Let me just grab it from the limousine—I'll be back in a flash." She walked over to the car and returned with a long, white box clutched in her hands. "This is for you, Ethel," she said. "Thank you for taking good care of our girl while we were in New York."

"Well, I had no idea..." Ethel said as she took the box from Blackwell. "Thank you so much! What a wonderful surprise!"

Blackwell held out her arm and checked her nails. "Believe me, it's my pleasure."

In that moment, just before Ethel started to open the box, my heart began to race. I saw Jennifer shoot me a sidelong glance filled with fear about what was to come next. I looked over at Tank as his mother did her best to work off the lid and saw in his eyes that he knew I was up to something. And then? Because of Tank's look alone, I wanted to back out—but before I could stop it from happening, the cover was off the box.

"Well, my word," Ethel said as she handed it to Harold. "Just look at this beautiful bouquet of flowers. They're so lovely. It appears to be a robust mix of what you'd find here locally, which is so thoughtful of you, Barbara. Thank you!" With a smile plastered on her face, she started to lift the bouquet out of the box. "You really shouldn't have," she said. "I mean, I'm just not deserving."

"Oh, I highly disagree," Blackwell said. "You deserve all of it, Ethel—you *really* do!"

When the bouquet was released from the box, I saw the lilacs hidden in the center of them. But Ethel—if only because she was so caught up in the moment of receiving a gift—didn't see them at all. Instead, she just closed her eyes, pressed the bouquet straight up against her nose, and breathed in deeply as she smiled a blissful smile. She breathed in their essence once more before her eyes slammed open as panic overcame her.

"Oh, no," she said as she sneezed. "No, no, no! Not lilacs! I'm terribly allergic to them. I break out into hives because of them! And my lips and face will start to swell—I'm sure of it!" She tossed the bouquet onto the gravel pavement with such force that some of the petals blew off and fluttered around our feet. "This is terrible!"

"But they're just an early summer bouquet," Blackwell said. "Everything in that arrangement is having its moment right now in gardens everywhere!" She sighed. "I thought you'd like them."

"Like them?" Ethel said in horror. "*Like them?* My lips are already starting to swell! I can feel them tingling. And my eyes are beginning to burn, which means they'll soon be shut tight!"

"I had no idea," Blackwell said, forcing empathy into her voice. "I just wanted to give you flowers. How awful. So sorry."

"You're starting to get hives, Ethel," Harold said. "I can see them popping up on your neck like a bunch of rubies."

"That's because I have fragrance allergies!" she said in despair. "And lilacs are *pure poison* to me! By tonight, I'll look like a horror show. And by tomorrow? On the day of my son's wedding? I'll be at my unrecognizable worst! How could this have happened? How?"

And then she looked directly at me.

"You did this," she said accusingly.

"Excuse me?"

"When we chose your bouquet, I told you not to go near a whole host of flowers, such as lilacs, lilies, daisies, and geraniums! I told you what they would do to me. How they could *destroy* me!"

"Do you honestly believe I'd remember any of that?" I said. "Good God, Ethel, Barbara only gave you that bouquet out of kindness! There's no need to make her feel worse than she already does."

"I'll be fine," Blackwell said, stifling a yawn.

"Ethel," Harold said in alarm. "Your lips are starting to inflate."

"Ub corb theyb are!" she said in despair. "Amb they're just going to get bibber."

"Holy sheet," Epifania said. "Look at them grow! They starting to look like those inner tubes my family and I used to get into this crazy country!"

"I suggest Benadryl," Blackwell said as Ethel started to dart up the stairs. "If you don't have any, let us know, and we'll get you some from one of the stores we passed by on the way here."

But by the time she'd said that, Ethel had already staggered up the stairs and flown into the house, likely in search of a medicine cabinet. She was gone, and in the wake of her hasty absence, I had to admit the bitch had had it coming to her. And even though Tank might question me about it, at that moment, I didn't care what anybody thought. What mattered more to me was what Ethel had tried to do to Tank and me. She deserved what my friends and I had delivered to her, and I didn't feel one ounce of guilt, second thoughts, or concerns.

In fact, I felt nothing but triumph.

18

LATER THAT AFTERNOON, after the caterers had arrived and I'd spent time with my parents while Tank visited with his uncle Sam and his cousin Taylor, who were two of his groomsmen, Tank joined me in our bedroom as I was removing my wedding-rehearsal dress from the closet. It was a sleeveless Oscar de la Renta beaded V-neck dress in plum with bright-red floral appliqués. It fell to midcalf on me, and I thought it was stunning as I laid it carefully down onto the bed. I'd also wear it to dinner, which would immediately follow the rehearsal itself.

"Hi," I said.

As he shut the door behind him, he looked down at the dress. "Is that what you're wearing at the rehearsal?"

"It is."

"That's some dress."

"Wait until you see my wedding dress."

"Tomorrow," he said as he came over and took me into his arms. "Or, if you'd like, you could always give me a peak at it now."

"No way," I said as I looked up at him. "Not only is that a

bad omen but I want you to see me in it for the first time when I leave the tent and start to walk toward you. Bernie is going to summon the gods so that I look my best for you tomorrow."

"But who's going to have my back?" he asked. "Who's going to make sure that *I'm* on point? Because it won't be my mother, I can tell you that. I'm not even sure she's going to make it to the rehearsal let alone to tonight's dinner."

I pulled away from him. "Is it that bad?" I asked, feeling a rush of guilt overcome me. It wasn't the first time I'd had second thoughts about what I'd done to her. As the hours passed since Ethel had become a bloated, hive-ridden wreck, I'd started to feel that I'd gone too far. And worse— that I couldn't go into my marriage with a lie between me and my future husband.

"It's pretty bad," he said. "But I think the Benadryl is starting to work. Her lips have stopped swelling, even though the hives don't look like they're going anywhere soon—they've covered her neck and face. Making matters worse is that Benadryl makes you feel stoned. We have a couple of hours to go before the rehearsal and the dinner, and she's still insisting that she'll be at each. But I'm not sure. We'll see what happens, I guess."

And that was enough for me.

"Tank, I'm the one who's responsible for what happened to your mother," I said, not willing or able to lie to him. "I knew she was allergic to lilacs. I planned everything."

"I know you did," he said.

He knew? Oh, for fuck's sake! And what now?

"How did you know?"

"Because I could see it on your face the moment it happened. You're not as skilled at concealing your secrets as you think you are, Lisa, so remember that in the future, OK?

Also, just so you know, I don't blame you for what you did. After what she said to you yesterday, my mother deserved what she got. All along, she's been trying to break us up, and look what she got for her efforts—first the tape, now the flowers. Let's hope she's learned her lesson."

Stunned, I just looked at him. "How do you know about the tape?" I asked.

"Yesterday I heard you two going at it in the library."

"But you were upstairs in the shower when that happened."

"When you were too long getting your glass of iced tea, it occurred to me that my mother might have entered the house. Since I knew you felt self-conscious about your appearance after we'd made love—and since I know my mother too well—I didn't want you to be alone with her without me. But when I came downstairs, I didn't find you in the kitchen. Instead, I heard both of you arguing in the library."

"What did you hear?"

"Enough to know that if I'd gone in there—which I almost did—things would have gone to shit in a second, and I'd probably never speak to my mother again—or she to me after she heard what I'd wanted to say. I wanted to take her on, Lisa, but in the process, I also knew that if I did, I'd fuck up our wedding day. So, while I stood there weighing my options, I listened. And as I listened, I knew that by taping her and then threatening her with that tape, you'd just cornered her. I've never been so proud of you as I was in that moment, because my mother's knowledge of that video is powerful. As ridiculous as she is, she's no fool. She knows that video can forever be used against her, and that alone has put the fear of God in her when it comes to crossing you again. Trust me on that, because you and I both know she'd never want me to hear it. She'd never want me to see her for who she really is."

He took me into his arms and said in my ear, "What you did kept this family together. What I would have done would only have blown it apart. So, thank you for having the guts to stand up to her again. I apologize for everything she's put you through—and I'm sorry she might never see in you what I see. But my father sees it, and I'm grateful for that. Because of the way you handled his wife, he will at least be able to see his son get married. And that wouldn't have been the case if I'd gotten involved, Lisa. My father would have been a gentleman and taken his wife's side, even if he disagreed with it. He wouldn't have come to the rehearsal, to the dinner, or to the wedding."

Before I could speak, he took my face in his hands, kissed me meaningfully on the mouth, and then smiled at me. "Thanks for coming clean with me."

"I had to. I acted out of anger and asked my friends to be my allies, and because they love me and were angry for me, they assisted me. I owe you an apology, and I also owe one to Blackwell and Jennifer. I was so angry with your mother that I felt victorious when she took hold of those flowers. But since then, I knew I couldn't get married to you without coming clean with you first. Tank, what I did was wrong—"

"I disagree," he said, interrupting me. "Look, Lisa—big picture, OK? Yes, my mother will look like a mess for a couple of days, but she's lucky. She'll recover from her allergic reaction to those lilacs. But if you hadn't done what you did, what would have become of us? Would *we* have been able to recover from *her*? I don't even want to think about that, so I say that she deserved it. She's been shut down—she now understands just how far you're willing to take things with her, and because of that and the tape, I don't think we're going to have to worry about her again."

"Do you think she knows that I'm behind the lilacs?"

"Oh, yeah," he said. "She totally knows."

"Fuck. Did she say anything to you?"

"She can't exactly speak right now, but her eyes told me she knew. And there was fear in them—fear of you."

"But that's the thing," I said. "I never wanted her to fear me. Jesus, Tank!"

"She brought it on herself, Lisa. Karma kicked her in the ass. What you need to know is that I'm fine with it, because my mother needed a wake-up call." He gave me another kiss and then slapped me on the ass. "But that's enough of that," he said. "You and I have a wedding rehearsal to go to and then a rehearsal dinner to attend." He nodded toward the bathroom. "So, how about if we get showered? You know —together."

"I love you, Tank."

"I know you do, Lisa—you show your love for me, and for us, time and again. I'm just happy that my mother hasn't frightened you away, because that would have killed me."

"Not happening," I said to him. "Come tomorrow, you'll be stuck with me for the rest of your life."

"I wouldn't have it any other way," he said. "Now—let's take that shower."

"Why do I think we won't just be showering?"

"Because I'm also marrying you for your intelligence. Now get in here."

With a wild sense of relief, I did.

~

WHEN IT CAME time for the wedding rehearsal, Ethel

McCollister was a no show, which was either a sign that she truly was ill—or that she was punishing Tank and me for what I'd done to her.

I wasn't sure, and I really didn't care.

Because the lack of her presence and her judgment made the proceedings go more swiftly and smoothly than they would have under her watchful glare.

With the help of our priest, Father Harvey—a tall, kind-looking man with a shock of white hair and a quick wit I liked at once—we went through the rehearsal twice while our friends either participated or looked on from the front row of seats. After an hour or so, we had it down, and it was nearly time for the dinner itself.

"Tomorrow's going to be quite the something!" I heard Epifania say.

"Tell me," Blackwell said, "exactly when do you plan to learn proper English?"

"Probably when you land yourself a man, lady."

"Then I guess I shouldn't hold my breath for that to happen anytime soon."

"Why sell yourself short?"

"Darling, please—it's the men I'm selling short, not me."

After Tank and I thanked Father Harvey for his help and guidance, Tank started to speak with his father, Alex, and his groomsmen while I went over to confer with Jennifer and Blackwell, who were sitting in the first row of chairs.

"You look fab," Blackwell said. "*J'adore* the dress."

"Of course you do," I said. "You're the one who picked it out for me."

"Which is why *j'adore* it."

"I need you both to listen to me while I have the chance."

"How positively mysterious of you..." Blackwell said.

"This is serious. Please listen."

I told them that Tank knew everything.

"*He knows?*" Blackwell asked. "Perfect. Because of your loose lips, now I'm in the goddamned doghouse when it comes to him. Thank you for that, Lisa. Consider my wedding gift to you revoked."

"He's not angry at all," I said. I looked over my shoulder and saw that Tank had his arm around his father's shoulders while Alex laughed and clapped him on the back. They were still happily engaged, which allowed me more time than I'd thought I'd have. "Let me tell you how it went down, which will clear everything up for you."

And so I told them. Everything.

"Well," Blackwell said. "I do admit that right now things don't look quite so bleak."

"Tank's amazing," Jennifer said. "He always has been."

"Nothing short of a prince," Blackwell agreed.

"I'm glad you came clean with him, Lisa," Jennifer said. "It was the right thing to do."

"My conscience got the best of me, as it always does. As time passed, I knew I had to tell him, if only because I couldn't go into this marriage with this massive lie hanging between us."

"You're right," she said. "You couldn't. But I'm glad he has your back. I'm glad he sees his mother for who she is."

Blackwell narrowed her gaze at me. "This isn't over yet," she said. "What if dear Ethel doesn't show for the rehearsal dinner—or the wedding itself?"

"I can see her skipping the dinner," I said. "I mean, we all got a good look at her when she ran into the house. But after several doses of Benadryl and a good night's rest? She'll be at the wedding."

"You see, I'm not so sure about that," Blackwell said. "In

fact, I think you need to prepare for the worst—not for the best—when it comes to this. I agree with the dinner—after the three of us cast the black plague upon her, I can see why she wouldn't come. But if Ethel chooses to skip the wedding, she'll only be doing so to underscore her contempt of you and her disapproval that this wedding is even happening. If she goes that far, just think about what Tank's friends and family will think of you then, especially when she's already warned many of them against you, like her sister, Margaret."

"What are you saying, Barbara?"

"Isn't it obvious? If she doesn't show tomorrow, you are going to be scrutinized and vilified by a hostile crowd on your wedding day, especially if Ethel is sitting in her bedroom right now working the phones in an effort to poison her friends and family further against you. I'm not telling you this to frighten you, Lisa. I'm telling you this so you can be prepared for any fallout. Ethel McCollister doesn't strike me as a woman who likes to lose, and the only thing she has left in her arsenal is the power of influence. You and Tank will get married tomorrow as planned, but I have to wonder under what conditions—especially if she plans to throw you straight under the bus."

19

When we retreated to the tent closest to the house, Harold went inside to check on Ethel, telling us he'd be just a moment. When he returned, it turned out that Blackwell had been right. Through him, Ethel had sent her regrets that she sadly wouldn't be coming to the rehearsal dinner or the wedding due to her "questionable health."

"Forgive me," she'd written on a card Harold read to us as we sipped glasses of champagne, "but my severe allergic reaction to those flowers has struck me down to the point that I've become bedridden. Please know that I wish my son and his bride the best tonight and tomorrow. I'll be thinking of you with only the warmest of thoughts."

"My mother the martyr," Tank said angrily, reaching for my hand.

We were standing just inside the tent, which had been festooned with a host of towering flower arrangements on cloth-covered tables and lit with soft amber lighting from the antique bulbs strung above us. Since there were only sixteen of us—actually, fifteen without Ethel—I'd chosen to go with a massive round table placed in the center of the tent so all of us could dine together instead of sitting at smaller separate tables. Soon, servers from the catering company we'd hired from Lincoln would start to offer the hors d'oeuvres.

"She's playing us, Lisa," Tank said. "Don't let her get to you, because I'm not. If she doesn't show tomorrow, that will be a stain on her for the rest of her life."

I told him about Blackwell's concerns.

"She could make things very uncomfortable for us," I said to him. "Especially for me if she turns your family and her friends against me."

"I'll handle it," he said.

"How?"

"Let's not worry about that now. Just know that I'll take care of it."

"OK," I said. I lifted my glass of champagne to him, and we touched glasses. "Here's to our last night of being single," I said.

He sipped his drink. "And cheers to that. I only wish we'd done this sooner. But we're here now, aren't we? In a couple of days, we'll be in Bora Bora, and then we can plot out the rest of our lives together."

"I love you, Tank."

"I know you do, and I'm grateful for it. I only hope you know that I love just as much, if not more."

I looked up at him, saw the love in his eyes, and knew that he did.

Despite everything that's happened this week, Tank and I will be fine. We just need to get through the rest of it.

"Before the hors d'oeuvres and dinner are served, we should spend some time with my parents," I said. "They don't know many people here. I don't want them to feel excluded."

"Lead the way."

"Hi, Mom and Dad," I said as we walked over to them.

"Lisa," my mother said as she took me in her arms and hugged me. "I was just telling your father how pretty you look in that dress."

"How do you like yours?"

"I love it," she said. "But come on—what's not to love?"

My parents didn't have much money. And because so many of my friends did, I'd wanted her to feel comfortable at the rehearsal, at the dinner, and also at the wedding. Several weeks ago, I'd called her and asked her to go to Bergdorf's website. After some gentle coaxing on my part, together we'd chosen two dresses and two pairs of shoes.

"They're my gift to you," I'd said. "For always being there for me, especially when some mothers are never there for their children."

"You're talking about Jennifer now, aren't you?" she'd said to me.

"I am. I won the lottery when it comes to you and Dad. Jennifer wasn't so lucky. So please, let me spoil you a bit. It's the least I can do, considering all you've done for me."

And now, Gert—which was short for her full name, Gertrude—not only was wearing a lovely Carolina Herrera butterfly-print dress in white and gold but had gone on her own to a new stylist and requested her first professional color and manicure. With her blond hair curling just above her shoulders, I thought that now, at fifty, she looked more vibrant and alive than I'd ever seen her.

"You know," my mother said, "I don't think I've ever felt so glamorous—at least not since the day I married your father."

"I've seen the photos," I said. "You looked beautiful on

that day, Mom. And I'm happy that you like the dress. It looks great on you. How do the shoes fit?"

"I've never worn such footwear in my life," she said, raising her right foot so I could admire the gold Dior sandals on her feet. "I mean, look at them! They're amazing."

"They're as amazing as you are," I said.

"Allow me to second that," Tank said.

"Come here and give your future mother-in-law a kiss," my mother said to him. "Because Al and I are over the moon that you're about to become a member of our family, Tank. We couldn't have asked for a better son-in-law."

As Tank gave my mother a peck on each cheek and then turned to my father to shake his hand, my heart swelled. This is how our wedding should be—with people who were genuinely happy for us, not working against us. As I watched Tank interact with my parents, I was reminded that there were plenty of people here who not only were rooting for us but wanted only the best for us. By getting into my head, Ethel had distracted me from all the love that surrounded Tank and me now. And I couldn't allow her to do that, because despite her best efforts to make me feel otherwise, I was the luckiest woman in this room.

"How are you, Dad?" I asked as I moved over to him.

When he embraced me, I smelled the familiar woodsy scent of his cologne—which sent me back to my youth, since my father had always smelled like this. Albert Ward was my mother's age, but because he'd lost his hair in his twenties, he looked slightly older despite his cheerful face.

"Proud of my daughter," he said. "And happy for her. On the flight here, I got to thinking about all that you've accomplished since you and Jennifer left Maine for Manhattan. Look at the success you've had with your books. And now, look at the man you're about to spend the rest of your life with. You've never disappointed us, Lisa."

"I've tried not to."

"Well, you haven't. Not by far."

"Are you ready to walk me down the aisle tomorrow?"

"If you'd chosen someone other than Tank, I might have had my reservations. But I have none." He looked at Tank. "It's going to be my pleasure to hand my daughter over to you."

"That means a lot to me," Tank said. "Thank you, Al."

"Thank you. Now, look," he said, turning to me. "You two should mingle. Don't worry about your mother and me. We'll be walking around and introducing ourselves to everyone."

"I agree," my mother said. "Go and have fun with your friends. Scoot!"

"They're the best," I said to Tank when we stepped away from them.

"They are," he agreed. "I wish I had your mother."

"But don't you see?" I said as I wrapped my free arm around his waist. "Now you do."

HALF AN HOUR before dinner was served, Tank went to spend time with Alex and Cutter while I went over to talk with Jennifer and Blackwell. All had a glass of champagne in hand and were admiring one of the flower arrangements.

"Don't take too deep a whiff," I warned as I came upon them. "I can't have either one of you down for the count. Ethel is enough."

"She's a heathen," Blackwell said. "Announcing that she wouldn't show tomorrow was downright cruel."

"And ridiculous," Jennifer said. Tonight she was wearing a gorgeous red dress, her hair in an updo, and I thought she looked as graceful as she did stunning. "Still, after all she's put you through, Lisa, you're better off without her there—unless Tank feels differently. I mean, she is his mother, after all. Where does he stand?"

"He's angry," I said. "When dinner is over, I think he's going to have a few choice words with her. She's supposed to walk him down the aisle tomorrow. Who's going to do it if she won't?"

"I will," Blackwell said. "In fact, I'd be honored to."

"I'll let him know that, Barbara. Thank you for offering."

"It would be my pleasure, because as everyone knows at this point, I consider Alex and Tank to be my surrogate sons."

"Just like you're my surrogate womb," Jennifer teased.

"While that doesn't have the same ring to it, darling, I do appreciate the sentiment."

"Looky, looky, it's the cookies!" I heard Epifania call out. "Epifania about to crash your party!"

I looked over my shoulder as she started to come toward us, and I had to give it to her—Epifania had dressed appropriately for the event. Instead of looking like a sex siren, she looked fresh, pulled together, and chic. She was wearing a stunning Naeem Khan short-sleeved, fringed cocktail dress that fell just above her knees. It was gold, shimmery, and elegant, with a beaded front and a tiered silhouette that complimented her curves. As for jewelry, she only wore diamonds at her ears and a large diamond solitaire on her left ring finger.

Which caused my mouth to fall open when I saw it.

"Epifania," I said as she joined us, "is that what I think it is? Are you and Rudman engaged?"

"Oh, holy to the moly," she said with a thrill in her voice. "Yes, we are! But you weren't supposed to notice it just the yet. I been trying to hide it from you, because this *your* weekend—not mine! The attention should be on you!"

"I don't care about any of that," I said, giving her a hug. "I'm so happy for you! You've waited years for the right man to come along, and Rudman is the perfect man for you. I think all of us here would agree on that."

"He's totally the man for her," Jennifer said.

"I couldn't agree more," Blackwell said. "Rudman loves Epifania. Parts of me are still trying to process how that can be, of course, given her sordid past. But I nevertheless know that he does."

"Why you the fucking with me, lady?"

"That was a joke, and you know it," Blackwell said. "As I've told you before, I'm fully behind your marrying Rudman. Because he *is* the one for you. Anyone with a pair of eyes can see how much that man is head over heels for you."

"When did he propose?" I asked. "*How* did he propose? I want to know everything!"

"But I shouldn't talk about this now," Epifania said. "This your weekend, not mine."

"Spill it!" I said.

"Well...OK. I mean, if you want. It was super romantic," she said.

"Go on..."

"A couple of days ago, he asked me over for dinner at his apartment, just as he has a hundred times before. He gave away nothing. Zeep. Instead, it was just like any other dinner at his apartment. We had the drinks. We had the kisses. We ate the meal. And then he was suddenly on one knee, which surprised me! Because after the dinner, it usually *me* on *my* knees!"

"And there's that," Jennifer said.

"With him down there and looking up at me with those big blue eyes of his, I started to freak out inside, because Epifania no fool—she knew what that meant. After he tell me that he love me, he removed a leetle black velvet box from his jacket pocket and opened it. I saw the bling and the bam, and then he asked me to marry him."

"What did you say?" I asked.

"Oh, *Heyzeus Cristo*, this is where it get the embarrassing," she said.

"It's not embarrassing," Jennifer said. "Your reaction was honest, real, and sweet."

"I started to cry," Epifania said. "I said that of course I be his wife. Because Rudsy just get me. He understand me, which I know can't be the easy, but he does. I know in my heart that he in love with *me*—and not my money. And now? Now this girl finally off the market!"

"Have you set a date?"

"Not yet. Because my Rudsy and I are going to have the fun first! We're going to travel the world, we're going to buy a beeg new apartment that work for both of us, and then we set a date and get the married. Lisa, I want you to be one of my bridesmaids. And I also want the Black Death here to be one."

"How very kind of you," Blackwell said. "Allow me to wear my mourning dress."

"But what if we get married in the afternoon?"

"I don't mean that kind of morning," Blackwell said, polishing off her glass of champagne with a roll of her eyes. "Just consider me in, Epifania. That's all you need to know."

"Same here," I said.

"That the perfect," she said. "Epifania really the happy right now!"

And then she turned to Jennifer.

"Yennifer, I know I haven't asked you yet, but I hope that you'll be my matron of the honor."

"It would be *my* honor, Epifania. And here's the good news—after tomorrow, your matron of honor will actually know what the hell to do!"

AFTER A DINNER that provided our guests with a choice between filet mignon, scallops provençal, or a spinach-and-gruyère soufflé as well as a host of desserts, it was time for the toasts. Alex clinked the side of his water glass, cleared his throat, and stood.

"This is where things can get kind of interesting," he said to the group with a wry smile. "This is where the best man can have a bit of fun."

"Go easy on me," Tank said with a laugh.

"That's the thing," Alex said with unexpected seriousness. "That's easy for me to do." He looked at me and then at the rest of those sitting around the table before reaching for his glass of champagne and holding it at his side as he addressed Tank directly. "We've known each other for so long and have experienced so much together, there's almost too much to share, isn't there?"

Tank put his arm around my shoulders and nodded.

"So, when I got to thinking about how I should toast you tonight, I knew I could have gone for a few easy jokes about the times you and I used to hang out at dive bars before I met Jennifer, but then I nixed that idea. You deserve better than that, Tank. You deserve something meaningful. To give you that, I knew I had one hell of a challenge ahead of me, because I somehow needed to distill the essence of what makes you *you*. That turned out to be more difficult than I'd imagined, because you're more complicated than I think most people realize. Many view you as the strong-and-silent type, which you are. But for those of us lucky enough to know the *real* you, you're much more than that."

Alex paused to sweep his gaze around the table.

"When Tank came to me six years ago to work at Wenn as the head chief of security, I knew him then only as Mitch McCollister. And to this day, I can remember the first time I saw him. I was interviewing for the job and sitting at my desk, waiting for the next person to arrive, when this massive man walked into my office armed with one of the most impressive résumés I'd ever read. West Point grad. Marine. Former SEAL. It doesn't get any better than that, and I knew it. And so we talked for a bit. I asked him what was important to him in his life, and he told me that even though he was now a civilian, he still lived by the SEAL ethos. He said he viewed himself as someone who was willing to serve, whether it be his country or his future employer. He told me that his character and his integrity defined who he was as a man. And then he assured me that his word was his bond. Throughout the entire interview, he was direct and sincere. And frankly, when the interview was over, I just gave him the damned job right then and there— because I would have been an idiot if I hadn't."

The group laughed.

"Little did I know then that over the years he would become my best friend, a man I would look up to and know I could share anything with. It didn't take me long to understand that with Tank, my personal life would never be betrayed by him, which is something he's proved to me time and again—and something that hasn't always been true for me in my life. Being in the public eye—a life I never wanted but which I had no choice but to assume—I can't underscore enough how much that has meant to me. So, thank you, Tank. Thank you for being true to your word."

Tank smiled and nodded at him.

"Everybody in this room knows I'd be remiss if I didn't say there's just this kind of cool, effortless, quiet sense of calm about Tank," Alex said. "It isn't forced—instead, it's natural. I think those qualities must be the reason his war buddies nicknamed him Tank. Because he really is solid as steel, he is physically intimidating, and he always can be depended upon—especially in the most dire of situations, as too many of us at this table know. And now, here he sits on the eve of getting married to the little sister I never had, Lisa Ward, who stands as a long-suffering and exhausted testament that Tank doesn't move quickly when it comes to matters of the heart."

I laughed when Alex said that and leaned over to kiss Tank on the cheek.

"He's more careful than that," Alex said. "More respectful. He's waited to get married and to have a family, because in a world where values have often gone missing, values mean plenty to Tank. I think everyone in this room knows that because Lisa and Tank have taken their time to get to the altar, they'll be married forever."

At that moment, Alex lifted his glass.

"Cheers to you, buddy. I love you like a brother. And you've nailed it by choosing Lisa to be your wife. You've taken your time, you've made sure that she's the one, and what you've created is gold, man. So, enjoy it. Know that I'm thrilled to stand beside you as your best man and that I'll always be there for you as your best friend."

As everyone took a drink and started to applaud, I looked over at Tank with tears in my eyes and said, "That was amazing."

"That's Alex," Tank said, and when he said it, his voice was unusually thick. I rubbed his back, knowing that what Alex had said in that speech had not only moved Tank but also meant the world to him.

"Well," Jennifer said, standing and placing her hand on Alex's shoulder, "that's a hard act to follow, but I know that I can when it comes to properly honoring my girl."

She looked over at me.

"Friendships," she said. "The real ones are hard to come by, aren't they? They are, especially the ones you know will last a lifetime. I once heard somebody say that people come in and out of our lives for a reason, but what's also true is that some of them remain in your life *for* a reason. I'm lucky to have a few friends in this room who I know will be with me until the day I die, and like Alex's friendship with Tank, I take none of them for granted—least of all my friendship with you, Lisa. We've known each other since we were children. If you stop and think about it, we've literally been there to witness almost all of our life experiences together, which astonishes me, because how many friends get to experience that kind of history together? Not many. But we have, and because we have, I've had the pleasure of watching you grow into the powerful, successful, fearless, fiercely funny, lovely, and wonderful woman you are today."

I put my hand over my heart when she said that, and I forced myself to keep it together as she took her own glass of champagne and held it at her side.

"Since we've been friends for nearly thirty years—which makes us twenty-five for those of you who are counting, Daniella—it's hard to know where to begin when it comes to our friendship and which stories to share with everyone. There are just too many. So tonight, I thought I'd take a few moments to share what it was like when Lisa and I left Maine and first arrived in Manhattan. Because if we hadn't taken that scary leap together, Lisa wouldn't be here with Tank now—on the eve of their wedding, no less—and I wouldn't be here with my beloved Alex. Our decision to leave Maine turned out to be so significant in how it changed our lives that it still stuns me. Lisa, think about how the ripple effect of that move alone swept us off our feet. I met Alex. You met Tank. But before they came into our lives, things always weren't so bright for us, were they?"

"No," I said to her. "They weren't. You and I struggled."

"We did, but we always had each other's back, didn't we? When I couldn't get a job for the life of me, you especially had mine. That's something I've never forgotten. It's just one of the reasons I'm proud to be your friend and your matron of honor."

I watched her look out as she addressed our friends and family.

"When Lisa and I first arrived in the city in her beloved car, Gretta the Jetta, her career as a writer was just taking off. During our second week there, she self-published her first horror novel on Amazon, and it sold so well that she immediately started to write another. I can't tell you how proud of her I was during that time, because more than anything, Lisa has always wanted to write for a living. Skip forward three months and a hell of a lot of hard work later, and Lisa was on the cusp of putting out her second novel while I was still trying to find work. At that point in my life, there literally was a bomb attached to my bank account that was set to explode if I didn't find a job soon. With money running out, I told Lisa I'd probably have to move back to Maine. But she wouldn't hear of it. At one of the lowest points of my life, she stepped in financially and kept us afloat until I finally found that job at Wenn. It's because of her belief in me that I was able to stay in Manhattan, which led me to Alex, the love of my own life."

When she said that, she appeared overwhelmed for a moment, and I watched her take a breath before she continued.

"Lisa, I want you to know that words aren't enough to express my gratitude for what you did for me back then. Your belief in me and your complete selflessness when it came to our financial situation are directly responsible for the life I now enjoy with my husband and our son. Because if I had gone home, I never would have met Alex, which is unthinkable to me. It's because you insisted that I stay—and that you'd take care of us until I found a job—that I was able to meet him, fall in love with him, marry him, and give birth to our son. What you did for me was so profound and generous, I'll never forget it. Never. I love you, Lisa. And I wish you and Tank a lifetime of mad love, happiness, health, and many, many children."

We both had tears in our eyes as she lifted her glass of champagne to me, and our friends and family members followed suit.

"Cheers to you," she said as she blew me a kiss. "*Love* to you. My *heart* to you. Know that I wouldn't be here today without you. I don't think you'll ever know just how much you mean to me, but I hope that after today, you will at least have a good idea."

I was so overwhelmed by what she'd just said to me that I got up from my seat. Tank encouraged me to go over and get her, and I hurried over and hugged Jennifer with a fierceness I felt in my soul. Together, we'd done it. Together, we'd triumphed. Only because of our friendship were we where we were today—happy, lucky, and in love.

"Thank you," I said in her ear. "What you said was beautiful. I love you, Jennifer. Where would we be now without each other in our lives?"

"I don't even want to think of it," she said as I felt her tears touch the base of my neck. "In fact, I don't *ever* want to know. But we did it," she said, pulling back to look at me with a big smile on her face. "We really did it, Lisa. We made it. Tomorrow is full circle for us. Once, we were just a couple of Maine girls with a dream, but despite all the odds stacked against us, we did it. Whoever could have known back then that we'd be where we are now?"

"No one," I said.

For a long, happy moment, we looked into each other's eyes and absorbed the significance of how we'd gotten here. Then Jennifer planted a firm kiss on my forehead and held me close to her again. "Later, let's celebrate as we always celebrate," she said in my ear. "Because when it comes to us, I can think of no better way to do that than to enjoy a martini with you."

"One that's as smooth as silk and as cold as January?" I asked.

"When it comes to us, is there another kind?"

20

On the day of my wedding, I awoke with a start.

"What's the matter?" Tank asked sleepily.

I quickly checked the time on the clock on the bedside table, saw that it was only five in the morning, and I rested my head back onto my pillow with a sense of relief. "Sorry," I said. "I keep thinking I'm going to oversleep."

He flipped onto his side and faced me.

"Excited?" he asked.

"You don't even know how excited I am."

"Ready to be my wife?"

"As Daniella would say, 'I'm totes to the ready for that shit to happen.'"

"And I'm totes to the happy to hear that."

I giggled as he swept me into his arms and kissed the base of my neck.

"This is really it," I said.

"It is," he said.

"We are so doing this today."

He started to kiss me on my shoulder. "We are."

"Sometimes I ask myself how I got so lucky. How someone like you would even want me for a wife."

He stopped kissing me when I said that and turned my chin so I could look at him.

"Don't you think I feel the same? Because I do, Lisa. Alex got it right last night. I've waited to get married, because I plan to marry only once. It took me years to find you. You are and always will be the love of my life."

"And now I'm going to cry again," I said. "I mean, Jesus, you'd think I was on my frigging period or something, because when am I ever *this* emotional? But I have been all week, and it's not just because of *that* reason."

"It's because of the wedding," he said. "And also because of my mother's treatment of you. In fact, it's probably mostly because of her. You've been under a lot of stress, and I'm sorry about that. I wish I could have been here to block you from it. At least from her."

"You couldn't have been," I said. "You had to go to Brian's funeral. You couldn't *not* go. I wanted you to be there for him and his family, and I'm glad that even though you lost your friend, at least you got the chance to say a proper goodbye to him."

I turned onto my side and faced Tank.

"Last night, before I came upstairs, you said you were going to speak to your mother. But you were gone so long, and—likely because Jennifer and I had two martinis too many—I wasn't awake when you came into the bedroom. What did she say? What happened between the two of you?"

"I didn't talk with my mother," he said.

"You didn't? But I thought that's what you were going to do."

"I decided against it. I decided she didn't deserve my

time. Instead, I talked with my father. We went into the parlor, and I told him everything. And at the end of it, I asked him what he would do if he were in my shoes. I asked him for his advice, which he gave to me."

"Are you saying that he knows about the tape?"

"He does."

"Oh, God. Tell me he knows nothing about the flowers."

"I didn't go there."

"Your father is no fool, Tank. He knows."

"And if he does, I don't think he gives a damn, because he was angry as hell last night after I told him what you'd been through with her since you arrived here."

"What did he say?"

"He said that he was sorry for the way Mom has treated you. He said that he tried his best to be there for you while you were here but that because of his responsibilities with the farm, he couldn't always be. My father isn't blind when it comes to his wife, Lisa. He knows what she's capable of. In the end, he said there was a good chance Mom wouldn't go to the wedding, that her pride was so great that she wouldn't walk me down the aisle, despite what that would do to our relationship. He said that all of this would be her loss and that he'd be there for me, even if she wouldn't. He's furious with her. He's pissed that she tried to hijack us, especially when we'd decided to get married here after she pretended to be excited for us. He didn't say these exact words, but he's pretty much calling bullshit on his wife right now, and he wanted me to let you know that he supports us and loves us regardless of what Ethel thinks."

"I've come to love your father," I said. "He's been wonderful to me since I've been here."

"He feels the same about you. He knows you're the one for me."

"So, if Ethel isn't going to walk you down the aisle, will it be Blackwell? I told you last night that she'd be happy to do it."

"While you were asleep, I phoned her last night after talking with Dad, and I asked her if she would. She said she'd be honored to. She also said that the dress she'd chosen to wear for the wedding would be 'perfectly suitable' to walk me down the aisle."

"What are your family and Ethel's friends going to make of this, Tank?"

"I really don't care what any of them think, Lisa, and you shouldn't either. Today is about us. I'm serious about that."

"I tried with your mother," I said. "I worked hard to make her like me. I need you to know that. Because I did give it my all—until her words and her deeds became so offensive, I couldn't take it anymore."

"Her actions are her own, and she owns the consequences. I don't want her there today. My mother might have given birth to me, but after what she's tried to pull when it comes to us? That alone doesn't give her the right to see her son get married. Some of us are lucky to have had great mothers in our lives while others are lucky to have had great mother figures. Barbara is the latter for me. So, she's the one who will be at my side today. Now, look. I've made my decision, and I'm happy with it. Today, we not only go forward without my mother but we do so knowing we have my father's full support."

21

Four hours before our noon wedding, Tank and I had showered, dressed, and breakfasted with his father. Ethel remained silent in her bedroom.

Whatever, lady, I'd thought at the time. *Your refusal to show your face this morning and to apologize to your son and to me says it all. You've made your choice. You've actually decided to miss your own son's wedding, and by doing so, you've also refused to walk him down the aisle. You might not know it yet, but those decisions will haunt you for the rest of your life.*

After we ate, Harold asked one of the farmhands to take our clothes down to the tents. Since my dress, his tux, and our shoes were sealed in heavy plastic bags, there was no chance they'd get dirty on the walk there. I was cleaning up with Tank at the kitchen sink when I heard the sound of cars pulling into the driveway. I looked through the sun-filled windows in front of me and saw the three limousines curling to a stop in front of the house.

"Those will be your friends," Harold said. "Lisa, I have a feeling that Barbara and Bernie are going to want to start turning you into the princess you're about to become. You should join them now so that none of you will feel rushed." He turned to his son. "It's probably best for you to join Alex, Cutter, and Rudman in your tent. Your uncle Sam and cousin Taylor will be along soon, and I'll direct them your way when they arrive."

"Thanks, Dad," Tank said.

"No problem." And then Harold just looked at each of us and addressed the elephant in the room. "I was hoping Ethel would come to her senses and join us while the three of us were having breakfast, but she hasn't, and since I know her like the back of my hand, if she isn't here now, she won't be coming to the wedding. I'm sorry about that."

"Don't be," Tank said. "That's her choice, Dad. But I'm glad you'll be there for us. I know you'll probably take some heat for that, but please know that Lisa and I appreciate your support."

"I wouldn't miss my son's wedding for the world," Harold said, and when he said that, the expression on his face became so deflated by defeat—if only for an instant before he caught himself—I could tell that he couldn't believe his wife would go this far in an effort to punish her son. But she had, and I could tell just by looking at Harold that this particular pill was hard for him to swallow. He was embarrassed by his wife's behavior, and my heart went out to him because of it. Ethel was Ethel, and not even her husband of so many decades could sway her from her decision.

"Now, listen," he said with a bright clap of his hands. "I know Ethel was supposed to be the one coordinating everyone's arrival, but in her absence, there's no reason why I can't see to all of it, so I will. I'll tend to everything—the cake, the caterers, and the guests. I don't want you two worrying about a thing, so how about that? Sound good?"

At that moment, I heard footsteps coming toward us.

"That won't be necessary," Ethel said. "Not if my son and his bride will have me, at least."

In surprise, I turned to my right and looked down the long hallway that led to the kitchen. And there was Ethel herself, walking straight toward us in a beautiful pale yellow dress that came just to her knees and emphasized how slim and fit she was. She was in full hair and makeup, and in her right hand was a large yellow hat. As she stepped into the kitchen and stood before us, I saw that with the exception of a few lesions on her neck, which she'd mostly concealed with makeup, that her face appeared normal to me.

"Ethel," Harold said.

"Would you mind tending to Mitchell and Lisa's guests, dear? I have some apologizing to do."

"It's too late for that," Tank said to her. "Nobody here wants to listen to anything you have to say."

"Let her talk, Mitch," Harold said. "Let her say her peace."

As Harold went to the door and told everyone that we'd be just a moment, Tank stood silent before he finally turned to me. "Do you want to hear this? Because neither of us has to."

"I think we should, if only for the sake of the family," I said, and that was true. After everything Ethel had done, she was on the brink of losing her son. And despite everything, I didn't want that to happen. I didn't want this family to be divided if Ethel could somehow turn it around now. Given her treatment of me—and her betrayal of us—I wasn't sure whether that was even possible. But since I was curious to know what she had to say, I looked at her, saw a rare look of vulnerability in her eyes, and then nodded at her.

"What do you have to say, Ethel?" I asked.

She put her hat down on the breakfast table and then seemed to search for the right words.

"That's just it," she said quietly to us. "I've behaved so poorly, I'm not sure quite what to say other than I'm sorry for my behavior and for how that behavior has affected each of you. I've had a day to think about this, and what I can tell you is that I'm ashamed of myself. I did some awful things that I'll never be able to take back, but I want you to know that I would if I could. Last night, from my bedroom window, I could hear the festivities coming from the tent below. And so I opened the window and listened to Alex's toast to you, Mitchell, and Jennifer's toast to Lisa. What they said was beautiful and heartfelt, and because of my own actions, I missed out on witnessing those moments in person."

She looked at me.

"The problem isn't you, Lisa," she said. "It's also not your books. You've done nothing wrong. If anything, you tried your best to put up with me until it was impossible to do so. The problem is me. It begins and it ends with me. If you were anybody else, I likely would have done the same thing to them. The question is why. Why have I done this? I thought about that this morning, after Harold chastised me for my behavior. By doing so, he forced me to face myself, which is why I'm here now. I obviously have an irrational fear of losing my son to someone else. I have my theories as to why that is, which are too personal to share, too difficult for me to revisit that time in my life. But as I thought about it this morning, I knew I couldn't use what happened to me when I was young as an excuse for how I've behaved. Because if I did, I would only lose everything I hold dear to me."

She's talking about her miscarriages, I thought. *And as awful as it is that she went through them, she's right—they are no excuse. They happened too long ago to use them as an excuse.*

And so I had to wonder. Was she being sincere right now? Should I believe what I was hearing? Or was she just manipulating us again? I wanted to believe her—I wanted this to be over between us—but I couldn't be sure. Was it possible ever to trust her again?

"I know that I have to change," she said. "And I'm ready to change—it's why I'm here now, dressed for the day and ready to help in any way I can to make certain that today goes as smoothly as possible for each of you. I don't deserve your forgiveness, but I'm hoping each of you will give me a chance to redeem myself." She looked at Tank. "And that you will allow your real mother to walk you down the aisle. Because I do love you, Mitchell. I hope that you and Lisa will allow me to mend what I've done."

"I don't know what to say," Tank said.

"That you'll give me that chance?"

"You went too far," he said. "You crossed too many lines. You tried to interfere with my relationship, for Christ's sake. That's a lot to swallow, Mom. You pushed me to the point that I actually didn't give a damn whether you came to our wedding today. Think about that for a minute."

"I don't know what else to say other than I'm genuinely sorry."

"I think you might be," I said—and when I said that, Tank looked at me in surprise. But then I knew more than Tank knew about his mother's past and how it had clearly fucked her up. That wasn't for me to reveal—I'd promised Harold to keep it secret, which I'd honor. But after listening to everything she'd just said to us, it was hard not to believe that Ethel had taken a good look at herself this morning. Maybe she had come to realize the consequences of her actions. Maybe she'd finally had her come-to-Jesus moment.

"I forgive you," I said. "But if you meddle in our lives again, Ethel, that's it for us. You need to be clear on that."

Her eyes welled with tears when I said that, and she quickly swiped them away, as if the act of showing emotion were something to be ashamed of. "Thank you," she said. "I understand why my son loves you—it's because you're good, Lisa. You're kind. I'm sorry for what I've done."

"What's this about your past?" Tank asked. "What happened to you in your youth that would drive you to behave as you have? I need to know, since it's clearly affected you enough to hurt the woman I love...and also me."

"I can't," she said.

"Well, you need to," Tank said.

"Ethel, it will be all right," Harold said from the doorway. "Maybe you should tell him. There's no shame in it."

"But I've never wanted to tell anyone," she said. "Only you know, because you had to know. And you'll never know how much I hated disappointing you then, Harold. How *humiliated* I felt each time it happened."

"Each time what happened?" Tank asked.

Ethel looked over her shoulder at her husband, and Harold nodded at her to go on. When she turned back to Tank, she tried to look at him but couldn't.

"Before I gave birth to you, I had two miscarriages," she said. "My doctor told me that I'd never have children. It's then that I found God. It's then that I started to pray. The reason I believe so strongly in my faith is because God delivered you to me, Mitchell. It was a difficult pregnancy, and I was ordered to stay in bed for months, but I still prayed...

right up until the day you were born. I can still see my doctor's face when she delivered you to me. She said it was a miracle, and I agreed with her, because I knew that you were in fact a miracle. When I first held you in my arms, I was so scared of losing you that I promised you that no one would ever hurt you. That I'd protect you for the rest of your life. When you decided to go into the marines, I thought I might lose you then. When you went to war, I was certain I might lose you. And ever since you went into personal security, it's been hell for me, because I nearly lost you several times while you were on the job. One time you nearly died for Lisa. You took a bullet for her. Would you take another one for her? Yes—of course you would, because you love her. And if not her, then you would have done the same for someone else, and then one day you'd be gone."

"Jesus," Tank said.

"I'm sorry," she said. "I've already told you that it's no excuse. I never wanted to share any of this with you. I just wanted to come down here and see if we could somehow start over."

Tank was silent for a moment before he came to his decision. "We can try," he said.

When he said that, Ethel looked up at him with such gratitude, I actually felt for her, because in her eyes, I could see all that she was feeling—happiness, shame, relief, and embarrassment. Was she being truthful with us now? It felt like she was, and for the first time in a long while, I wondered whether we could eventually put all this behind us and become a family.

That was my hope, but I already knew that I'd forever be wary.

"That's all I ask," she said to him. "Will you accept my apology?"

"I'll accept it for now," Tank said.

"As will I," I said. "Because believe it or not, Ethel, I do want this family to be close. It would be great if we could become friends one day. Whether that happens is up to you, not me."

"That's more than fair," she said.

I checked the time on my watch and knew I had to leave and join my friends, if only because I didn't want Bernie to feel rushed. He not only had to do my hair and makeup but also Jennifer's, Blackwell's, Daniella's, and Alexa's.

"I need to go," I said to Tank as I stood on tiptoe to give him a kiss on the cheek. "Everyone is waiting for me." In an effort to lighten the God-awful mood that hung in the air, I said to him, "I'll try to be a princess when you see me next."

"And I'll do my best to look like your prince. Have fun with Bernie and the girls, OK?"

"And you have fun with the boys." I looked over at Harold and hooked my thumb toward Tank. "You'll make sure this one looks his best?"

"You can count on it, Lisa."

"I know I can, Harold." And then I looked at Ethel, who seemed lost to me, as if she felt uncomfortable in her own home. Her own skin. After all that she'd just said to us, I decided to reach out to her again in an effort to take the weight off her. "And I'll see you at the wedding, right?"

"You will," she said.

"Tank, will Ethel be walking you down the aisle? I'll need to tell Blackwell."

"Do you want to?" Tank asked his mother.

"More than anything, Mitchell."

"Tell Blackwell that I appreciate her willingness to step up for me but that my mother will be walking me down the aisle."

"Will do." I looked at Ethel. "I'm glad you're coming, Ethel. Thanks for seeing to everything while we get ready."

"It's my pleasure, Lisa," she said. "It really is."

And when she said that, the gratitude in her eyes alone sold me.

The woman meant it.

22

"How ABSOLUTELY, SPECTACULARLY, POSITIVELY MELODRAMATIC," Blackwell said once I'd told everyone what had just transpired in the kitchen. After greeting one another in the driveway, we were now walking toward the tents and the gazebo. The morning was hot and the sun was blinding, but at least there was a breeze, for which I was grateful.

"Oh, it was every bit of that!" I said.

"That *mujer* is kind of a whack job," Epifania said. "And when I say the whack job, I don't mean the hand job, OK? Because just so you know, my leetle tribe of the boobies, I never confuse the two!"

"Noted," I said with a giggle.

"Lisa, I think you handled the situation as well as you could," Jennifer said. "I mean, walking through that mine-field and deciding where to step couldn't have been easy."

"What a lovely metaphor," Blackwell said whimsically. "And not at all a cliché."

"Lady..." Jennifer warned.

"Oh, lighten up, Mommie Dearest. I'm trying to brighten

the mood. I mean, look at me, for heaven's sake. A goddamned trooper walking through a never-ending path of grass while trying to dodge a motherlode of mud pies. And in Dior heels, no less. If that doesn't score me a few points, I don't know what will. I mean, in this heat, it will be a miracle if we get to that tent alive, so we might as well have a few laughs along the way—only so that if we do die, and rigor mortis sets in, the people who come upon us will say, 'Well, at least they died smiling.'"

"You know," Jennifer said, "actually *that* was absolutely, spectacularly, positively melodramatic."

"Oh, my dear!" Blackwell said. "It's still early—and I've just gotten started!"

"Mud pies," I heard Alexa say behind me in a weirdly dreamy voice. "Do any of you have any idea the sheer amount of nutrients that are in them? I know most people just see them as nothing more than piles of manure—"

"Shit," Daniella corrected. "Piles of cow shit, Alexa, because that's what they are. Don't try to frame them as something they're not."

"Fine, cow shit," Alexa said. "But you should be thankful for them, Daniella, because you've certainly benefited from them."

"What does that mean?"

"Since I've only seen cattle and chicken being raised here, I have a feeling the McCollisters sell their manure to other farmers who grow things like wheat, which is common in the Midwest. And since I know you love yourself one big pile of spaghetti, what you should also know is that the wheat that produced that spaghetti was likely nourished with huge quantities of cow shit. So, think about that for a moment."

"I think we're all thinking about that at this moment," I said.

"You're telling me that the noodles I eat are made from shit?" Daniella asked.

"I'm telling you that they *benefit* from the nutrients in it. Jesus, do you really know nothing of substance at this point in your life?"

"I know you're a closeted lesbian."

"And here we go with that again," Alexa said. "Whatever."

"One day, I can totes see you being the leader of Dykes on Bikes."

"Lovely," Alexa said. "And should that ever happen, I'll be looking out for you in your group. You know, Whores on Wheels."

"Hilarious."

"Girls..." Blackwell said.

"Oh, come on, the Barbara, don't spoil thees leetle sheet show right the now!" Epifania said. "Because thees sheet is starting to get the good!"

"Lisa?" Bernie called out.

"Yes, Bernie?"

"Do you happen to know the name of that hot-looking cowboy I saw back there a few moments ago? You know, the dark-haired one? The one who was leaning against one of the barns and who needs to have my fingers running through his hair later today? He was wearing Levis and chaps as if he was about to go to a leather bar."

"A leather bar?" I said.

"Yes, a leather bar. He was wearing them hiked up to the hilt in an effort to show off his beguiling bulge. Naturally, seeing him like that has spiked my interest."

"Define 'spike'," Blackwell said.

"You already know what I mean, woman," he said in an oddly husky voice.

"And this stirring I believe you felt," she said, "it happened without the Viagra? Without the magic of those little blue pills, you still managed to get an—"

"I did," he said. "And no blue pills were needed when it came to laying my eyes on *that* one."

"*Mon Dieu!*"

"*Je connais...*"

"Are you talking about Phil?" I asked Bernie.

"Is that his name?" Bernie said. "Because if that *really* his name, then all the better."

"You're incorrigible."

"I just want his number. Certainly you can supply me with that. You know, so I can *sext* him!"

"That's not going to happen, Bernie. Sorry. If Ethel ever found out, she'd likely freak out—just when I need to keep her in check."

"Sexting," Daniella said. "*J'adore* it, as Mom would say. Cutter and I sext all the time."

"Even at work?" Jennifer asked.

"Will I get him in trouble if I tell you we sext ourselves senseless while he's at work?"

"I think you just admitted that's exactly what you do."

"No, I haven't. I was simply asking."

"Daniella, come on. You can't be sexting Cutter at work. You know that."

"Fine, then. We are not sexting at work."

"Oh, my God, they are," Jennifer said to me. "And how gross is that? Sometimes I think Cutter is just answering a text, but it could be something else. It could be her—and he could be aroused!"

"Please!" Blackwell said. "Try being her mother. The things I'm forced to hear from *that* one on a daily basis..."

"At least you don't hear me when I rip out a rapid succession of queefs," Daniella said.

"You did *not* just say that," Alexa said.

"I did—and without shame. Because Cutter is big down there. When we make love, I make all sorts of unnatural noises. They even surprise me."

"It like you're the farting, right?" Epifania asked. "But only not from your leetle hoo-hoo. Instead it from your leetle meow-meow!"

"Yes! Thank God *you* understand me, Epifania. It's like a part of me is farting in places where I never should fart."

"Well, good for you, my leetle *chiquita*. Because you not the kidding. That means that Cutter really does have a whopper!"

"Are we seriously having this conversation?" I said. "On my wedding day?"

"We totally are," Daniella said. "I mean, look at Tank, Lisa. With a man that size, certainly you've sent your share of queefs into the world."

"I'm not going to answer that."

"You shouldn't," Alexa said. "Because it's disgusting. Are we really meant to hear this? I mean, come on, Daniella—at least have some sense of common decency."

"Cutter and I are in a committed relationship," she said. "And besides, I thought that sharing our lives was a completely open book when it came to this group. We tell each other everything—always have. Tell me if I'm wrong."

"You're wrong," Blackwell said. "At least when it comes to *those* kinds of details. If that's all you're going to talk about, Daniella, you need to shut it."

"But I love hearing about a big cock," Bernie said.

"Well, of course you do, Bernie—but this is my daughter. Please try to understand."

"Cutter has a big cock, Bernie."

"Details!"

"There will be no details, Bernie. Daniella, that's enough."

"And he totes knows how to use it."

"I will disinherit you if you keep this up."

"Fine," Daniella said. "I'll stop...now that all of you know the truth of Cutter's big cock."

"You are such a vapid size queen," Alexa said.

"Said the woman who's only experienced another woman flicking her clit with her tongue."

"And that's just something I don't need to hear right now," Jennifer said.

"It's a reality when it comes to that one," Daniella said.

"Oh, give me a break," Alexa said. "You know that isn't true. And even if it were true, so what? Humanity is way more complicated than you can wrap your sorry little mind around, Daniella. Some men are attracted to men, like Bernie."

"Hear, hear!" he said.

"And some women are attracted to women—"

"Like you," Daniella said.

"And the rest of us are attracted to the opposite sex."

"The rest of us," Daniella said mockingly. "As if you are the rest of us, Alexa. You can't pull your old Levis over these eyes. Because I'm on to you."

"You're a tramp," Alexa said.

"And you wish you were wearing denim and flannel to the wedding."

"Well!" I said to everyone as we approached the tent. "Here's the good news—we're finally here." But before we stepped inside, I turned and faced them. "And thank you for that," I said.

"Thank us for what?" Blackwell asked.

"For trying to make me laugh on the walk over here."

"Is that what we were the doing?" Epifania said in confusion. "I thought we were just the walking and the talking. You know, there was the part about the queefing, which Epifania totally understand because my Rudsy been known to give my leetle meow-meow the hiccups. And then we talk about how Alexa belong to the Dykes on the Bikes, which all of us just accepted as truth because what else could we do, you know? I mean—look at her. And then we learn that Daniella eat the sheet for the dinner, which frankly was just the gross. Other than that, I thought it was a good conversation."

And she really believes that, which is one of the reasons I love her.

"Anyway, thanks for getting me in a better mood, because parts of what was just said were as funny as they were horrifying—and I needed that right now."

"Were we that transparent?" Blackwell asked.

"You were," I said as we stepped inside the air-conditioned tent, so cool that it was a welcome shock. "But I appreciate it."

I looked at Bernie.

"Ready to turn me out?" I asked.

"You know?" he said. "After seeing Phil, I feel oddly inspired. But I want you to come last, Lisa. Alexa and Daniella just want me to blow out their hair. Jennifer and Barbara want something a bit more detailed. So, let me tend to them first, and then I'll have at you so that when you leave here, you'll be at your freshest."

"Do we have time for all that?" I asked.

"Plenty of time," he said. "Because without Phil in my life, this queen is officially on a mission to chase away the blues. Now, I need all of you to just step the hell back and let me at it! Because right now...watch and learn, ladies, because I'm about to become a fucking magician."

23

THREE HOURS LATER, behind a private partition that had been set up for all of us at the rear of the tent, I stood before a long mirror and just looked at myself as I listened to Bach's *Arioso* playing outside the tent and Jennifer and Blackwell made certain that my dress fit perfectly.

"Lisa," Jennifer said when she took a step back, "you're so beautiful. Tank isn't going to know what to do with himself when he sees you like this."

"He isn't," Blackwell said, "because let's just face it—this gown, that hair, and that makeup of hers are a goddamned triumph. As for the dress, thank God for Chloe at Bergdorf, because without her help, we never would have gotten our hands on what has come to be known as the rare and coveted Vera Wang Galilea wedding gown. Wang only made five of them this year—and at eighty grand a pop, the greedy little bitch. But it is divoon, isn't it, my love? Worth every cent. I mean, just look at how well it fits," she said as we locked eyes in the mirror. "The halter neck. The macramé lace. The sheer French-tulle back. The delicate, hand-embroidered veil. It's beyond stunning—and then there's what Bernie did to you. He gave you the 'loose and the low' style favored by Gigi Hadid, which is absolutely on trend right now. And then there's your makeup—so bright and polished. You look like a princess. You really do. And by the way, my dear, I have to commend you for not caving in to that 'something new, something old, something borrowed, something blue' bullshit. Because right now, you need none of that."

"I don't even recognize myself," I said. "I mean, I know it's me, but it's kind of like I've been photoshopped. I never knew I could look like this."

"This is you at your best," Blackwell said. "And that you chose to wear only your diamond engagement ring was the right choice, because that's the one piece of jewelry everyone should be focused on today. I say brava! Well done! Perfection! Champagne?"

"My nerves are so fried right now, I could really use a glass—but I'll pass. Because as both of you know, Tank and I are winging our vows. We decided that when we say them to each other, we wanted to be in the moment and to hear what comes from the other's heart."

"How very daring of you," Blackwell said. "But also so romantic. Do you know what you'll say?"

"Look, I'm no fool—I have rough idea, but that's all I need. When I look at Tank and say my vows to him, I will say exactly how I feel about him and us at that moment."

"How very Philippe Petit of you," she said.

"Who?"

"Philippe Petit. He was before your time, but in the midseventies, he walked between the Twin Towers on a tight rope. The towers are gone now, of course, which still devastates me due to the friends I lost there. But the courage he displayed by walking that rope reminds me on some level of what you and Tank are about to do—going into your vows without a safety net."

"I just hope I'm coherent."

"You will be," Jennifer said. "You are a writer, after all."

"Of zombies."

"There is that," Jennifer said. "But you'll still be great."

"Shall we show the others how you look?" Blackwell asked.

"Let's," I said. "But before we do that, let me take a moment to look at both of you."

While I'd asked all my bridesmaids to wear something sophisticated and elegant in the palest of pinks for the wedding, it was agreed that since Jennifer was the matron of honor, her dress needed to rise just slightly above the others, which it did in a host of subtle ways. It was well-known a rule that no one should upstage the bride, and Jennifer, Blackwell, Alexa, and Daniella hadn't. Jennifer was wearing a Carolina Herrera sleeveless grid-illusion midi dress in a light, lovely pink. Bernie had given her a dramatic updo. And because I'd decided to wear only my engagement ring, Jennifer had followed suit by just wearing her engagement and wedding rings.

I thought she looked flawless.

As did Blackwell, which was no surprise to anyone who knew her. She was wearing something that didn't quite have the drama that Jennifer's dress had, but it was chic as hell. With Chloe's help, they had reached out to Gucci months ago to see if they could give Blackwell and her daughters different variations of their short-sleeved Cady Cape dress, complete with a ruche detail down the front neckline with half-pear studs. Each dress was just different enough to allow Blackwell and her daughters the individuality they wanted while still being part of a planned, cohesive whole.

"Lisa, your Mom and Dad are here," Alexa called out. "They said you only have ten minutes to go. Epifania has already left to sit with Rudman. All of us will need to walk down the aisle soon. You need to get in here *now*."

"Oh, God," I said. "This is really happening."

"It is," Blackwell said. "And fast—and at last."

AFTER ALEXA, Daniella, and Blackwell had left to walk down the aisle with the groomsmen they'd been paired with, Jennifer turned to look at me just before she left to join Alex.

"How are you?" she asked.

"I think I'm starting to have an anxiety attack," I said.

"Seriously? Or are you just joking? Don't mess me with now, Lisa. Because this is happening, and I need to leave to meet Alex. Are you OK?"

"I'm good," I said after taking a deep breath. "Nervous, but good. So...go. And thank you for everything, Jennifer. I'll see you in a moment."

"First let me fix your veil," she said as she quickly adjusted it. "There, now you are perfect. And I'm gone. You've got this," she said to me. "I know you do. I love you."

And then she went straight out of the tent with her white roses held closely in front of her—and looking every bit the star that she was.

For my bouquet, I'd gone with a simple clutch of sunflowers, as bright as the day—and which Tank had been surrounded with in this very meadow when he was growing up on the farm. Ethel had shared that bit of information with me when we were at the florist—when she'd made the fateful mistake of pointing out everything she was allergic

to. "But these sunflowers?" she'd said to me at the time.
"These will take him back to his youth. They'll remind him
of the meadow in fall. These will mean something to him."

And so I'd ordered them, hoping that they would.

As I watched Jennifer reach for Alex's hand and start to
walk toward the gazebo to Debussy's *Clair de Lune*, my father
came up behind me and put his hand on my shoulder.
"Right now, it's my duty to tell you that you don't need to go
through with this wedding. So, you don't need to go through
with this wedding, Lisa. That said, are you ready to go
through with this wedding?"

I smiled when he said that and then I nodded. "More
than anything, Dad."

"Your mother and I are proud of you," he said. "You and
Jennifer found good men to spend the rest of your lives
with. Your mother and I will love Tank as if he were our
own son."

"I appreciate that, Dad," I said, hugging him. "Thank
you for always being there for me."

"Is it time for us to go?" he asked.

I peered out of the tent and saw Father Harvey
ascending the gazebo's steps. "I think this is it," I said.
"Father Harvey is there now. People are looking around in
their chairs for us. We should go."

"Then...let's go."

I hooked my arm through his—and off we went.

When we left the tent, the first thing I felt first was the
hot sun against my skin, the oppressive heat pressing
down upon me. Then I felt the energy suddenly directed
straight at me, because when Dad and I had started
toward the gazebo, people began smiling at us and taking
photos with their cell phones, which I didn't expect at all.
Because of Ethel's influence, I had been expecting to face a

mostly hostile crowd, which was one of the reasons I'd felt so nervous a moment ago. But as we walked down the carpet and passed our guests, hostility was the last thing I felt. If anything, I felt that people were happy to see me. That they were ready and eager for this wedding to take place.

Did Ethel somehow get in front of this?

I had to wonder, if only because I'd heard what she'd said on the phone to her sister, Margaret, which had been nothing short of an indictment of me. I also knew that she'd influenced others against me. After I'd left the house this morning to join my friends, had she somehow found the time to make a rush of calls in an effort to turn things around for Tank and me? Or had she already done that before she came downstairs to apologize to us?

Whatever the case, she must have done something, I thought as my father and I moved forward through a sea of smiling faces. *Maybe there's hope for us after all, Ethel...*

As I leaned into my father for support, I looked forward and saw Tank beaming at me as we drew closer to him. As I faced him, he was standing to the right of Father Harvey, with Alex and the rest of his groomsmen beside him. I felt a rush of love for him when I saw him.

He looks happy, I thought as I smiled at him. *He looks as excited as I feel right now. And just look at how handsome he is in his tux—could he be any hotter? No. How can this be my life? How can it be that I'm lucky enough to get married to such a kind, smart, brave, and generous man?*

After Dad and I ascended the stairs and I saw that Blackwell actually had tears in her eyes—and that Jennifer was happily joining her—I nearly lost it right then and there.

And would have if Father Harvey hadn't suddenly spoken.

"Who presents this woman to be married to this man?" he asked just loudly enough for everyone to hear.

"Her mother and I do," my father said.

"And so it is done," Father Harvey said, nodding at my father to take a seat after I'd given him a kiss. In a daze, I stepped beside Jennifer and watched my father descend the steps to join my mother in the front row. When I looked at her, she gave me a discreet wave before she put her hand over her heart.

"We gather here today to unite these two people in marriage," Father Harvey said. "Tank and Lisa's decision to marry has not been entered into lightly, and today they publicly declare their private devotion to each other. The essence of this commitment is the acceptance of each other in entirety, as lover, companion, and friend. A good and balanced relationship is one in which neither person is overpowered or absorbed by the other, one in which neither person is possessive of the other, one in which both give their love freely and without jealousy. Marriage, ideally, is a sharing of responsibilities, hopes, and dreams. It takes a special effort to grow together, survive hard times, and be loving and unselfish."

He asked Tank and me to face each other, which we did.

"Do both of you pledge to share your lives openly with one another and to speak the truth in love? Do you promise to honor and tenderly care for one another, cherish and encourage each other, stand together through sorrows and joys, hardships and triumphs, for all the days of your lives?"

"We do," Tank and I said in unison.

"Do you pledge to share your love and the joys of your marriage with all those around you, so that they may learn from your love and be encouraged to grow in their own lives?"

"We do," we said again.

And then Father Harvey asked Jennifer and Alex to come forward to present the rings. As each black velvet box was opened, the profound meaning of this moment shuddered through me. In a matter of seconds, Tank and I would officially become husband and wife—and I felt overjoyed, as I knew that Tank did as well. Because when the rings were presented by our friends, he locked eyes with me—and I saw them brighten with unexpected emotion. After all these years—and after all we'd gone through together—this was it.

"May these rings be blessed as a symbol of your union," Father Harvey said. "As often as either of you look upon these rings, may you not only be reminded of this moment but also of the vows you have made and the strength of your commitment to each other." He addressed our guests. "The bride and the groom have chosen to deliver their own personal vows to each other. Lisa and Tank, please step forward and face each other."

We did.

"Tank," Father Harvey said. "Please share your vows with Lisa. She—as well as your family and friends—will stand as witnesses to them."

"That would be my pleasure," Tank said to the priest. When he faced me, he looked me directly in the eyes. My pulse quickened and my mind whirled at how quickly this was proceeding. I now remembered what my mother had said to me just before she'd left the tent.

Remember this moment, she'd urged. *Never forget it. I know it's going to be overwhelming and emotional, but try your best to relax as much as possible and to take in as much as you can. You'll thank me later. I love you, Lisa.*

And so I focused just as Tank began to speak.

"Lisa, standing before you today is right where I want to be," he said. "And if there's anything I can be certain of in the future, it's that I will always have you with me. It's been over two years since I asked you to marry me, and I'm thrilled that today we finally will become one. From this day forward, my heart will be your shelter, and my arms will be your home. I vow to give you my loyalty and my eternal heart, because you are the only woman I will ever need."

He shrugged at me.

"How can I ever make you as happy as you've made me?" he asked. "How can I ever make you laugh the way you make me laugh, especially since your sense of humor is one of the things I love about you most? What I can promise you is that I will try. For the rest of our lives, I'll also try to make certain that you'll always know you are the most important person in the world to me. We chose each other, and I need you to know that this is the best decision I've ever made in my life. Ever since we first fell in love, you've been my foundation, my sounding board, my eternal source of motivation. That is why—in front of all our family and friends—that I promise to support you unconditionally. I will cherish you for as long as I am able. I love you, Lisa, and I cannot wait to begin our lives together as husband and wife."

I was so moved by Tank's vows that my eyes welled with tears, and I wondered if I had the strength to get through my own vows to him. But when I looked up and into Tank's eyes, all the strength I needed was right there waiting for me to take. And so I took it. And in that unconditional moment of love that passed between us, I knew then everything I wanted to say to him.

"Tank," I began. "I'm here today to promise you that I will love you for eternity. You are one of the bravest and most remarkable men I know. You are also my best friend—

my true soul mate. After all this time, I'm still captivated by your selfless, humble, caring, and respectful nature. Thank you for your unwavering support for my career over the years, and thank you for making me feel loved, even when sometimes it's seemed undeserving. Most importantly, I want to thank Jennifer for bringing us together, because when she first introduced us in the lobby of our old apartment on Fifth, I was taken by you right then and there. At first, the attraction was physical. But as we got to know each other, it came to be so much more than that. As I stand here today, I truly believe that I'm the luckiest woman in the world. My vow to you is that I will always support your dreams and will express my love for you for the rest of our days together, even when we are apart. I will never take our union as husband and wife for granted. I will always love you unconditionally, Tank, for better, for worse, for richer, for poorer, in sickness and in health, and until death do us part—even if you should somehow turn into a zombie. Because if that should happen, I think we all know that I'll still love you and that I'll likely have a perfectly sound strategy to bring you back alive to me—where you must always belong. I love you, Tank. I love you to my core."

After we exchanged rings and Father Harvey pronounced us man and wife, he asked Tank to kiss his bride. To my surprise, it wasn't just a peck on the lips Tank had in mind. Instead, he literally swept me off my feet, dipped me low, and then planted one mother of a kiss on my lips. Happily, I kissed him back.

"I love you," I said in his ear before he let me down.

"I love you so much, Lisa. Thank you for agreeing to be my wife."

When Tank gently placed me back onto the gazebo's floor, I caught a glimpse of Ethel in the crowd and saw that she was looking at us while wiping tears from her eyes. She nodded at me at that moment, I nodded back at her, and then I watched Harold place his arm around his wife's shoulders in such a loving gesture that I knew I was watching a man who had taken his own vows seriously. Despite all that Ethel had done—and regardless of the reasons why—he was there for her now. And because of the kindness he was showing to her alone, I couldn't help but feel touched.

"Go now in peace and live in love, sharing the most precious gifts you have—the gifts of your lives united," Father Harvey said. "And may your days be long on this earth, together as one."

When our guests stood and erupted into applause and whistles, Tank took my hand, I squeezed the hell out of his, and we looked into one another's eyes. The enormity of this moment sent chills through me.

Together, we walked down the steps, at last man and wife. And as rice was tossed upon us as we laughed and walked up the red carpet with dozens of photographs being taken of us, I wondered in my heart if I'd ever feel as overwhelmed with happiness as I was at that moment. It was that perfect. It felt that complete.

And it was ours to relish forever.

EPILOGUE

Two days after Tank and I returned from our honeymoon in Bora Bora, Jennifer called to ask if I'd like to have lunch.

"Please tell me you're free this afternoon," she said. "I've given you two full days to settle in, and I can't stand it anymore. You've been gone so long—I've missed the hell out of you. Tell me that you're free."

It was nine o'clock, Tank was already at work, and I was just about to sit down at my computer to start my next book, which absolutely could wait for another day. "I'm totally free," I said. "And I'd love to have lunch—just tell me where, and I'll be there."

"How about if we go to Ruby's?" she said.

"Ruby's Diner? I can't remember the last time I ate there. Tank and I had our first date there."

"Alex and I used to go there a lot, but then for some

reason we stopped going. I've been feeling a bit nostalgic lately, so I thought we might go there today. Because I honestly can't remember for the life of me when I was last there."

"Same goes for me," I said. "But I'd love to go there again. Good on you for thinking of it. Count me in for the pure nostalgia of it all."

"Done," she said. "How about if you meet me at noon in Blackwell's office? Because when I told her yesterday that I was going to call you today for lunch, she made it very clear that she wanted to hear all about your honeymoon, as I do. Let's talk in her office for a bit, then I have a surprise in mind, and then we'll go to lunch."

"What surprise?"

"You'll see," she said. "But best to bring the Kleenex!"

"What does that even mean?"

"You'll see. See you at noon!"

JUST BEFORE NOON, I arrived by taxi at Wenn Enterprises with perspiration already shimmering along my forehead. It was sunny, hot, and humid in the city—the temperature had to be somewhere in the midnineties, which provided its own certain kind of hell—and even though the cab was air-conditioned, it was barely enough to fight off this day.

I paid the driver, thanked her, got out of the car, and dashed across Fifth Avenue's busy sidewalk and into Wenn's much cooler lobby. Even though I had dressed for the day in capris, a white tank, and pretty sandals, I felt as if my makeup were already melting down my face—which Blackwell wouldn't have.

And so, before I took the elevator to the fifty-first floor

where her office was, I went to a restroom off the lobby, dabbed my face with a paper towel, and removed a compact from my handbag to freshen my makeup. When I was confident I was Blackwell ready, I took the elevator to her floor, which was alive with people hurrying this way and that. Many of these people I'd come to know over the years, and I said hello to them before I arrived at Blackwell's door, which was open.

"Knock, knock," I said as I stepped into the doorway.

"And just listen to that," Blackwell said as she popped a cube of ice into her mouth and leaned back in her chair. Jennifer was seated in front of me and turned to look at me with a big roll of her eyes. "Already rife with the clichés, and yet she dares to call herself a writer."

And then Blackwell leaned forward.

"But let's play the game, Lisa. Shall we? Who's there?"

"Seriously?"

"Play the goddamned game."

"Fine. How about...a new bride?"

"Not good enough," Blackwell said. "So, allow me to correct. How about...a woman whose nipples are about to poke out poor Jennifer's eyeballs?"

"What are you talking about?" I said.

She pointed at my breasts. "Those."

I looked down and saw with a sense of humiliation the two tents in my tank. "I just came from ninety-degree heat," I said. "And then I stepped into Wenn's lobby, which is about forty degrees cooler. Give me a break."

"I think it's more than that. I think you're already longing for Tank again."

"You'll get no argument from me there, lady."

With a toss of her bob, she stood up and came over to give me a hug. "So, how was it?" she asked in my ear. "And don't be shy, because Jennifer and I want to know all of it. How was Bora Bora Bang Bang?"

"Really?" Jennifer said. "Bora Bora Bang Bang?"

"Please," Blackwell said. "I mean, just look at her. Aroused and ready to go. She looks like an order of takeout for the Internet porn crowd."

"I do not," I said.

"Trust me, darling, that was a compliment," Blackwell said as she walked back to her desk and sat down. "And you should take it, because I can only imagine how many men and women would pony up their credit cards to have a good look at you right now."

"Anyway," I said, sitting down next to Jennifer. "The honeymoon was amazing."

"Describe amazing in ways that has nothing to do with you flat on your back and Tank on top of you," Blackwell said. "Or with you on your hands and knees with him thrusting behind you. Because if you can come up with an answer to that question, I'll be surprised."

"Why?"

"Isn't it obvious? You were there for three full weeks, and yet you've somehow managed to return to us without a tan —which says it all to me. You and Tank eschewed the pleasures of the South Pacific and instead decided to spend your time focused on *your* South Specific."

"So what if we did?"

"Actually, I'm glad that you did," she said, the goading gone from her voice. "In fact, I'm thrilled that you did. Now, all joking aside, spill it. How was Bora Bora? Despite its inherently dull name, I've always wanted to go."

"It was magical," I said. "Before we rented our hut, I sent each of you a link to it online for your approval. And as nice as it looked in the photos we saw, it was way better in person. Our hut stretched about a hundred feet out into the ocean, and the waters there were so clear and blue, you could stand on the deck and see all kinds of fish swimming below. If they had better Internet, I'd consider living there."

"Without a Bergdorf?" Blackwell said. "Unthinkable. Already, you've lost me."

"The shopping is better than you think," I said.

"Really? Then give me names. Stores. Designers. Everything."

"It's not so much about the clothes," I said. "Instead, it's all about the jewelry you can find there. And I'm not just talking about diamonds or other gemstones that abound there. What I'm really talking about are the pearls, which just makes sense given the location, right? One day when Tank and I were out, I came upon what had to be the most beautiful pearl necklace I'd ever seen."

"Was this before or after Tank gave you a pearl necklace of his own?" Blackwell asked.

"You're disgusting."

"What I am is Blackwell—which is a name you now can search for on Google. Somehow I've become a goddamned Internet sensation!"

"That's all your ego needs," Jennifer said.

"Deal with it, girl."

"What did you two do for food?" Jennifer asked. "Did Tank cook in the hut, or did you mostly go out for dinner?"

"Let's just say that while we were there, Tank went all *Free Willy* on me. Since he was pretty much naked all the time, he mostly cooked for us in the hut."

"Well, goodness," Blackwell said. "I hope that hot grease didn't spatter onto him—and that he was careful when he used a knife."

"I made sure of it. But enough about me. Since I pretty much had zero cell phone connection while I was gone, I have no idea what's been going on here. How have you two been?"

"I've been great," Jennifer said after I saw her shoot Blackwell with a concerned, sidelong glance. "Aiden is happy and growing. Alex is over the moon when it comes to his son. And for the first time in a long time, there appears to be no drama surrounding Wenn. So, can we just celebrate that for a moment?"

"Agreed," Blackwell said.

"And how about you, Barbara?" I said, looking at her with new eyes. "How are you and the girls?"

"I'm fine," she said with a dismissive wave of her hand. "So are Daniella and Alexa. While Tank and you were having your naked adventures, the rest of us were clothed and leading more predictable lives."

"So...why did Jennifer just give you a weird look?" I asked.

"Did I?" Jennifer said, turning to me.

"You did."

"Look," Blackwell said. "Today is about you, Lisa. It's not about me."

"So, something *is* up," I said. "The three of us have always shared everything together, and we always know when something is off, as it is now. What's happened? What's the problem? I need to know."

"I really didn't want to talk about this today," Blackwell said. "But since I know that when you're like this, you become like a dog on a bone, I might as well just tell you now. Jennifer, would you please close the door?"

She did.

And when she did, Blackwell turned to me. "While you

were on your honeymoon, I lost one of my closest friends," she said.

"Barbara," I said. "I'm so sorry—how?"

"She was driving to work one morning when she was involved in a head-on collision. Her name was Miranda Hart. We became fast friends decades ago when we were in college, and we'd remained close ever since. But here's what I can't shake, Lisa—Miranda was only fifty-four. She'd been married for more than thirty years. And now not only is her husband in a state of shock but her three children are bereft without their mother. I'm not going to lie to you—it's been heartbreaking and terrible."

"My God," I said. "Barbara, I had no idea..."

"Of course you didn't, but now you know. I've always tried to manage these sorts of life events on my own, but this one has hit me particularly hard, especially since Miranda's children are close to the ages of my own children. What happened to her could happen to me—that's what I can't get out of my head. For so many years, I've been going through life thinking that I'm invincible, when clearly I'm not. Miranda's death has taught me a lesson—the cliché is true. None of us should take any day for granted, because in a flash, it can cruelly be stolen away from any of us."

She checked her watch, stood, and started to walk around her desk.

"Now, look, I don't mean to get all maudlin on you before you go to lunch, and I'll be the first to admit that I'm unusually emotional right now. But in the wake of Miranda's death, and whether it comes to my daughters or to Jennifer or you, Lisa, I'm finding myself facing the sudden end of things. Two weeks ago, that's what happened to Miranda's husband, their children, and their friends. Everything just ended. Everything just stopped."

She motioned toward her door.

"What if you two walk out that door and we three never see each other again? What if this moment is it for us? What if we've just had our last dance? Because none of us know whether that's the case. Our final memories of each other could end right here. So, before you go to a lunch I've likely just ruined—and I do apologize for that—please give me a hug before you leave and know that I love you both. And that I always will."

After Jennifer hugged her, I hugged her. "I'm so sorry," I said again, socked for a lack of words.

"As am I," she said as she pulled away from me. "But both of you need to heed my advice right now. All of us need to learn from my friend's untimely death, if only so that we can live our own lives to the fullest. I plan to start doing that now. I plan to spend less time at work and more time with my girls and my girlfriends. Because the eighty hours a week I spend here is beyond the call. I need to get a life. One day, I hope to have a relationship. In the wake of Miranda's death, I need to rethink everything. And as you and Jennifer go forward with your own lives, I hope you won't make the same mistakes I've made. Life isn't just about your careers. It's also about the relationships you hold dear. I plan to tend to that, I plan to celebrate them, and I plan to get better at all of it. Because I need to. And as careerists, I hope you and Jennifer will as well."

"My God," I said to Jennifer when we left Blackwell's office and moved toward the bank of elevators at the end of the hall. "What in the hell was that?"

"That was Barbara facing the fact that time is limited for

every one of us," she said. "And by the way, what you just witnessed was her emotional state two weeks *after* Miranda's death. I can't tell you how shaken she was by it when she first heard the news. She's actually much better now. In fact, it was good watching her be her old self when she first started sparring with you. She's coming back. I believe she'll make changes to her life, and I also believe she'll be back to her old self soon."

When we stepped into one of the elevators and started to descend, I asked her what surprise she had tucked up her sleeve for me.

"You'll see. Cutter is going to take us there first before we go to Ruby's."

"Why the mystery? You know I hate being kept in the dark. I was always the kid who raided the house a few weeks before Christmas so I'd know for sure my mother was nailing it with the gifts."

"I remember that," she said. "And I also remember that it led to plenty of sad faces when you saw that she hadn't."

"What my mother never understood was why I'd never want Barbie dolls when what I really wanted were Dracula and Frankenstein dolls."

"Actually, I think your mother got it when you started defacing your Barbie dolls. You know, when you crossed out their eyes with little Xs, stitched up their lips with black thread, and shaved their heads bald so you could use your bright-green crayons to expose what was supposed to be Barbie's toxic brain."

"My poor mother," I said, thinking back to those days. "What's so great about her is that she never discouraged me."

"That's because she was frightened of you." The elevator slowed, and the car doors slid open. "Let me text

Cutter," she said. "He'll bring the car around, and then off we'll go."

"But where?" I said as we stepped out. "And why did you ask me to bring Kleenex?"

"You'll see," she said.

"As you keep saying, which is irritating."

"Whatever," she said. "Let's go."

"Jesus," I said to Jennifer when Cutter pulled the limousine to a stop in front of our old apartment building on East Tenth Street, where we'd landed our first one-bedroom flat when we moved to Manhattan. "Look at it. I thought it looked exhausted back then, but check it out now. It's literally sagging in the heat. It looks like it needs watering."

"I don't know," Jennifer said with fondness in her voice. "Seeing it after all these years is kind of magical, isn't it?"

"Frankly, it's kind of magical that we got out before it caved in on us."

"Oh, come on," Jennifer said as she looked out the window at it. "Think about it. Everything started here for us. See that window there on the third floor—that's where you wrote your second book."

"All I remember is that we nearly died of heat exhaustion in that apartment. Do you remember how hot it was that summer? You know, before we scraped up enough money to buy that used air conditioner of ours?"

"The one that shook the windows?"

"That's the one."

"Well, it did the job," Jennifer said. "As did the rot-gut vodka we used to drink."

"Breakfast of champions."

"Do you have a favorite memory here?"

"I do."

"Tell me."

"It's the day we left this sorry dump and got our sweet new digs on Fifth with Blackwell's help."

She just shook her head at me in disappointment. "This was supposed to be a moment between us. Why aren't you taking this seriously?"

"Because I'm not the sentimental type?"

"I know better."

This clearly means something to her...but why?

In an effort to find out, I took hold of her hand. "Let's get out of the car," I said. "If we're going to do this, then we need to have a proper look at the old girl."

"Let's," Jennifer said. "Cutter, how about if you ride around the block? We'll flag you when we're ready to get back in."

"You've got it, Jennifer."

On the sidewalk, the two of us stood beneath the shade of a nearby maple tree and silently looked up at the dilapidated building we'd once called home.

"No wonder I write about zombies," I said to her. "I mean, come on. Once, I somehow felt at home here—and this joint is scary. It all makes sense to me now. First were the things I once did to Barbie, which were questionable at best, and then the fact that I was actually happy to live in this building, which has to be haunted."

"And yet we had fun here, didn't we?"

When she said that, I glanced over at her and thought back to those days, remembering how much fun we'd had here. I looked up at the windows of our former apartment and recalled how thrilled and scared to death we'd been the moment we first learned it was ours. It seemed like a lifetime ago to me, and yet it had been a matter of only a few years.

"We did," I said after a long moment. "We made the best of it, Jennifer. As wrong as this building is, at least it offered us a roof over our heads so we could try to make it here."

"That's the perfect way to put it," she said.

"Why are you suddenly so nostalgic?" I asked. "That's not like you. You've never lived your life in the rearview. Instead, you've always kept looking forward. What's going on with you? I'm confused."

"I don't know," she said. "I think what happened to Blackwell when you were gone also affected me. Because when it comes to our own story, Lisa, it feels like the pages have turned way too quickly. You and Tank are married now. Our lives have settled. We no longer are the two hustling broads who came here to make names for ourselves. Back then, neither of us knew that we'd end up where we are today. I guess I miss that raw kind of hustle."

"You sound almost regretful," I said.

"That's not what I mean. I'm grateful that both of us found good men. I'm over the moon that I have a son whom I adore and a husband I'll love forever. One day, you and Tank will start a family. And then our children will grow up together. Those are wonderful things that I hold dear. But back in the day, when we first came to live here? Sometimes I do miss the simpler lives we led back then, especially given some of the hellish events we've survived since. When you and I first arrived here, the energy was different—it was urgent. Electric. And it drove each of us to get where we are now. I wanted to come here today to celebrate what we've achieved. And also to thank you for believing in me."

"I've never *not* believed in you, Jennifer."

"Back then *someone* had to, and it was you, Lisa. You were

unwavering in your support of me. I'll never forget all that you did for me."

"Jennifer, you edited my books for me back then," I said. "And think of how much you've done for me since. You introduced me to Tank, for God's sake! You've literally changed my life."

"Don't you see?" she said without hesitation when she turned to look at me—and when she did, I saw that her eyes were lit with emotion. "I'd do anything for you. I'd do all of it again—and again and again. Thank you for being my best friend. Thank you for seeing me through to where I am today. Because I know for a fact that I wouldn't be where I am now without you at my side—or without you having my back."

She turned toward the street when she said that and started to look for Cutter as she cleared her throat. Before I could speak, she took my hand in her own without looking at me.

And in that moment, I chose to just look at her—and admire what stood next to me. Despite her past with her abusive parents, in the end, Jennifer had won. She'd proven herself to be a survivor. She'd fought hard, and she'd made it. She was one of the strongest people I knew, and I loved her for it.

A light breeze lifted her hair off her shoulders. She reached out and captured the stray tresses with her free hand while her other hand clutched tightly to mine. Sun dappled through the trees and lit her with a beautiful mosaic of light and color as people hurried past us on the sidewalk.

"I have one more surprise for you," she said, not looking at me.

"I'm not sure I can handle another," I said. And after all that had just transpired between us, I meant it.

"This one you can," she said when she turned to me. And when she did, I saw in her eyes the love she held for me.

"What is it?" I asked.

"I chose lunch at Ruby's for a reason."

"I get that now."

"No," she said. "No, I don't think you do. At least not all of it, because there's more."

"I don't understand..."

"Alex and I had our first date there—and so did you and Tank."

"We did," I said. "But what does that have to do with today?"

"Today is full circle for me," she said. "Now that you're married to Tank, today marks the beginning, the middle, the end, and the future for all of us. I hope you'll see today the way I do, because I've asked Alex and Tank to join us for lunch. The four of us will gather at Ruby's for a reason."

"To celebrate how far we've come," I said, now understanding the profundity of the moment.

"That's right," she said, and as Cutter rounded the corner, she held up her hand to grab his attention. He pulled toward the curb. "For me, with all of us sharing the same table together at that miraculous little diner that once seemed so insignificant to us, it now will stand as an exclamation point in our lives."

"We've never been there together," I said. "Not the four of us."

"Then let's be there together now," she said as she led me off the curb and toward the limousine as Cutter jumped out of the car to open our door for us. "Let's go and have lunch with the loves of our lives in the very place where love first touched each of us."

"Full circle," I said.

"That's right," she said as we greeted Cutter and stepped into the limousine's cool comfort. Before Cutter swept us away, Jennifer put her hand on my knee and then pointed at our apartment building. "Once, we were just two girls from Maine who came here with a dream. And look at us now. We did it, Lisa," she said. "Who would have thought?"

"We did," I said. "Because we didn't come here on a whim. We came here to fight and to win. But you're right, Jennifer. We did it. We really did."

She leaned forward and tapped Cutter on the shoulder. "Let's go to Ruby's, Cutter." She turned to me with a smile. "Because Lisa and I have a lunch date with our husbands."

AFTERWORD

Can't wait for my next book? More are on the way, and finding out when is easy! Join me here at christinaross.net and you also can find me on Facebook, where I love to chat with my readers. Just search for Christina Ross Author.

If you would leave a review of this or any of my books, I'd appreciate it. Reviews are critical to every writer. Please leave even the shortest of reviews. And thank you for doing so!

XO,
   Christina

Made in United States
Orlando, FL
06 August 2022

20594940R00143